RANGE

M. MCPHERSON

*To the party people of 1313,
My classmates that shaped me and my teacher that made
my writing into a story.*

To my past self who only saw the poisonous side of adults...

Your trauma wasn't in vain.

I

Fraser's eyes were glued to the grave in front of him. Its surface was smooth, not yet having been carved and yet it felt like there was a hole carving itself out of his chest.

"I'm sorry for your loss."

Grief made his muscles so stiff it made him immobile, yet he found himself straining his neck to see the person beside him. It was his dad, who looked as grief-stricken as him, his face was tight and his eyes shaking with restrained emotions.

"I'm so sorry for your loss."

Fraser couldn't respond to his father, his tongue lay numb, unable to ask why he was sorry and whose grave they felt so destroyed over. How important is this person that his father came out of his hometown to see them buried? Except his father hadn't left his hometown, a frantic glance around and Fraser noticed he was in his hometown. Who died?
As the question entered his mind, stone pieces fell from the grave stone as letters began to appear, his eyes widened as he watched the name make itself fully known.

"Wake up Fraser," his father mumbled. "This is none of your concern."

They were no longer alone. There were more voices, all telling him to wake up, yet when he glanced around there was no one there.

Wake up Fraser

Come on, sleepy head.

Wake up!

Fraser jolted awake almost smacking himself in the face to turn on his hearing aid. A glance around told him he was still on the plane, it had landed. Sighing, he focused on slowing down his racing heart as he moved a hand up to his face and smoothed down his hair.

"...thank you for flying with..."

The flight attendant's words drifted off as Fraser looked out the window and gazed at the gray overclouded sky. There were always situations like his, in movies or in books, where the main character had to move from places where sunshine always had a place to reach, to end up in a place the exact opposite. However, in Fraser's situation, it doesn't matter where the sun would dare shine, it's the people that made it bitter for him.

Passengers moved in the corner of his eye, letting him know that people were making their way off the plane, yet he didn't move an inch, the dream still wearing on his muscles. The clouds looked like they were going to burst with rain at any second and the wet concrete told him that it wouldn't be the first time.

He should've brought his raincoat so he wouldn't be soaked to the bone by the time he made it to his father's home. No, he threw away his raincoat, the memories etched into the fabric weren't worth staying dry. If he had enough money, he could've taken a cab, but he wasn't ready to touch the money his mother had left behind. The thought of hitchhiking came to mind, but it left as soon as it came. Knowing his luck, he'd become a victim of a serial killer.

The plane didn't have many occupants, so it didn't take long before Fraser became the only one sitting on the plane. He could've been mistaken for an old man as he slowly got up from his seat and reached into the overhead department to get his bag. He departed from the plane with a nod of thanks to the flight attendant and entered the airport loving the ear-piercing silence. The number of people contradicted the size of the airport though it wasn't a surprise. The airport is for the forgotten small towns that only a handful know about, if one were to look the towns up they wouldn't even show up on Google Maps.

"Fraser," a voice called, the only warning he received.

He was slammed into a warm embrace, arms were thrown around his neck, a head of golden locks blocking his view. It took him a moment to realize who it was and a moment longer for him to awkwardly wrap his arms around his Aunt Kimberly, bending down a little so her feet could touch the floor without struggle. He should've known she would be here to pick him up, she was always there for him when needed.

She kept him in a tight hug until he gently pinched her side, his way of letting her know that the hug had been going on for too long. Fraser wasn't a person for physical affection but was tolerant when it came to his Aunt Kimberly, however only to an extent. Aunt Kimberly slowly eased herself away from him, not yet ready to part from him. She took a step back and Fraser let out a quiet sigh of relief. He needed a moment to breathe.

Aunt Kimberly took the distance as a chance to give him a once over. He'd grown a head taller than her, and his hair had grown longer. He looks a lot like his father much to his irritation.

"O, I've missed you so much," she blurted. "It's been so long since I've seen you, you've gotten so tall and your hair."

She reached out to pull a lock in between her fingers and Fraser made sure to stay still, letting her twirl the strands between her fingers like she used to do when he was little.

"I've missed you too," he said truthfully.

Aunt Kimberly was one of the two people he regretted leaving behind and not keeping in contact with while he was away. He could see his aunt getting emotional and decided to steer the conversation.

"I see you've gotten taller," he teased.

Aunt Kimberly let him steer the conversation and put a hand on her hips, giving him a non-threatening glare.

"I'll have you know little man I'm a woman of average height and still tall enough to kick your butt."

He put his hands up in fake surrender and slowly backed away laughing.

"My apologies Aunt Kimberly."

She rolled her eyes and walked away. Fraser put his hands down and shoved them into his pockets, following her out the airport to a small parking lot. He sees his aunt's minivan and stops in his tracks. The last time he saw the minivan it was covered in a layer of dirt and had a rainbow sticker on the windshield. Now it seemed the layer of dirt was the best version of the car.

The dirt had been scrubbed off and the car had been painted all black but that's not what had Fraser at a standstill. It seemed the rainbow sticker wasn't enough, from the driver's door, wrapped around the car to the passenger door is a painted rainbow that began inches from the roof and ended just above the side mirror. If that wasn't enough there were children's handprints, each a color of the rainbow.

Aunt Kimberly unlocked the car and was just about to climb in when she noticed her nephew wasn't following.

"Fraser," she called out. "Are you getting in?"

He took a moment before dragging his feet toward the minivan.

"What happened to your car?"

Aunt Kimberly had the nerve to look confused.

"Who vomited rainbows on your car," Fraser asked, gesturing wildly to the kindergarten centerpiece.

She gave a sheepish smile.

"I may have let the kids give my car a little makeover."

"A little?" He raised a brow.

Aunt Kimberly laughed and ran her hand through her blonde hair, untangling the curls in the process.

"Okay more than a little," she amended. "Can we get in the car, please? It's cold outside."

The air was crisp, and goosebumps had already riddled up and down Fraser's arms and legs. Sighing, he reluctantly went up to the minivan and got into the vehicle. As he went to put on his seatbelt, he noticed the hulk and hello kitty stickers that were scattered up and down it. He pulls it out far enough for his aunt to see.

"Really?"

She glanced at the seatbelt as she pulled out of the lot and swerved down the road.

"The kids were feeling a bit under the weather, so I decided to let them decorate my car."

Fraser put the seatbelt on the second he felt the swerve.

"You let your class ruin your car," he clarified.

Aunt Kimberly smiled and shook her head.

"I let my class *decorate* my car."

He shook his head and began to pick off the offending stickers strapped across his chest.

"How under the weather were the kids that you had to resort to letting them 'decorate' your car?"

Aunt Kimberly's lips twitched trying to keep her

smile easygoing.

"The adults have been putting their underwear on a little too tight and it's been affecting the kids."

There was something else that she wasn't telling him, it was clear as day. Aunt Kimberly wasn't good at omitting the truth, that much hasn't changed. He could tell she didn't want to tell him the whole truth, but he wasn't going to push her.

"Well, if they're still under the weather why not let them over your house and have them decorate your walls?"

The look on his aunt's face made him laugh.

"I'm not that crazy Fraser."

The car swerved as a rabbit jumped out into the road. Aunt Kimberly jerks the wheel and Fraser smacks his head against the window flipping off his hearing aid. Aunt Kimberly rightened the car and let out a deep breath.

"Wow, that was a close one, wasn't it Fraser?"

He doesn't answer as her voice was overridden.

Welcome back

"Fraser!"

He reached up and turned his hearing aid back on, his heart pounding. Aunt Kimberly reached across the console to the passenger seat, laying a hand on his shoulder. Fraser jumped and looked at his aunt, her face had twisted up in concern.

"You okay?"

He nodded his head, his hand lingered on the switch of his hearing aid. Aunt Kimberly eased off the gas pedal and drove for the first time at the speed limit.

"You can still hear them?"

Her voice was no louder than a whisper as if she were afraid someone was to overhear her.

"I never stopped hearing them," he explained.

Aunt Kimberly opened her mouth to question him

further but the look on his face prevented her from doing so.

Since Fraser was young, he lost his hearing in his ears and not long after he could hear voices. They weren't voices of the living, but voices of the dead. Fraser didn't know at the time. As a child Fraser would talk to them without reservation whether in private or public. He would do whatever they wanted whether it was giving a message to a loved one or just giving them the conversation they had long craved for. At first, everyone took it as something child-ish that he did but when they realized he wasn't growing out of it, it became a problem. Adults and children alike avoided him and talked about him excessively. It got to the point where they held a meeting to discuss what they should do with him. His parents argued back and forth relentlessly until his father kicked both him and his mother out. He didn't want to deal with them, they were 'problems' he didn't want to solve. Luckily it all happened before the townspeople could get their hands on them.

"Don't worry, I'm pretty sure I'm the only one that remembers."

For a second Fraser almost let himself believe her, but a disadvantage of being born in a small town is that everyone remembers everything about everybody.

They made it to town in record time, thanks to Aunt Kimberly's lead foot. Fraser had also concluded that her lack of consciousness while driving is the reason his parents never let her drive him around town.

She whipped the minivan into the driveway and turned off the car the moment she put it into park.

"Here we are," she smiled.

Fraser looked through the windshield and gazed at his childhood home. It had been so many years since he was able to land his gaze on the house. It seemed to have lost its youth, the paint on the house and door had faded and the grass was dead. Why did no one take care of the house?

"What happened?"

Either she didn't hear Fraser, or she ignored him, he didn't know which, but his question went unanswered.

"Come on, let's go."

They got out of the car and climbed up the stairs to the front door. Each step had Fraser breaking out in a sweat, his nervousness appeared out of nowhere. By the time they got to the front door, he had to wipe his clammy hands on his pants. Aunt Kimberly didn't notice her anxious nephew and folded her hand into a fist before banging loudly on the door. They waited a few moments before Aunt Kimberly prepared her fist again, knocking on the door even louder. Nothing, no signs of life came from within.

"He's probably asleep," she guessed. "You know your father's a heavy sleeper."

Fraser didn't have the heart to point out that if memory serves him right, the drop of a pen could wake him up. His aunt prepared to put in all her strength to knock on the door when the door next door banged open.

"You gonna claim to be the police with how hard you knockin'?"

Standing at the door was the next-door neighbor, in a floral nightgown. Aunt Kimberly gave the neighbor a smile while Fraser couldn't help but stare. She seemed familiar to him, yet he can't quite put his finger on why.

"Good afternoon, Edna," Aunt Kimberly greeted with an extra large smile. "It's good to see you on this mighty fine day."

Fraser couldn't help but feel like his aunt was laying it on a bit thick. She was forever rainbows and smiles yes, but the stiffness of her smile gave off a different feeling.

Edna ignored Aunt Kimberly and looked at Fraser,

her gaze pierced a hole through him.

"You Andrew's boy?"

He paused then gave a timid nod. Something in his instincts was making him feel…unordinary in her presence. Fraser began to shift from foot to foot feeling the weight of her stare.

"Well, your father isn't home right now," she grumbled. "He's at work, so stop making all that ruckus."

Aunt Kimberly leaned forward a bit, wanting to ask when her brother would be home, but before she could utter a word Edna slammed the door shut and stomped off inside.

"She hasn't changed a bit," she sighed.

Fraser turned and gave Aunt Kimberly his full attention, leaning towards her, eager to ask a few questions.

"Has she always lived here," he asked.

Aunt Kimberly bent down and lifted the tattered welcome mat and pulled something from underneath it. It reflected off the light and he realized it was a key. Had they lived in a larger area, he might've been worried for his safety. Aunt Kimberly took a moment to process his question.

"Edna?"

He nodded and watched as his aunt used the key to unlock the door, smiling with satisfaction as it opened. She walked in like she was the owner of the place and after a moment of hesitation, he followed her inside.

"Yea, she used to watch you when your parents had a few…disagreements."

Disagreements? When Fraser's mother packed their things and left, it wasn't just his Father kicked them out and she took Fraser and left. They had tried to get him and the town to get along, making it seem like talking to the dead never happened but the town was already planning. Plan A was to send Fraser away to get the care that his parents couldn't give him. His mother fought tooth and nail to get rid of that idea, her child wasn't just someone who could be sent away because he was different. Next was Plan B, which was for him to meet up to the town's level of normalcy.

It worked for a while, Fraser stopped talking to the dead in both private and public settings, however, the voices of the dead were dangerous unanswered. No one likes to be ignored, whether it be the living or the dead, Fraser was being pestered by the dead, day and night. There were several things that were said that are ingrained into his brain even years later.

Do you think I'm just a voice?

It happened in the middle of class when he heard the voice ask the question. Had it not been followed by a dead person's hand pulling his hair, he might've made it. A meltdown that had students and adults alike scared was the final push the town needed to hold a town meeting. Not able to handle the pressure, his father kicked them out and his mother was none the wiser. Though Fraser never remembered going to his neighbor, Edna's house. When did that happen?

"Since your dad's not home we'll just hang out," she declared. "I'm sure he won't mind."

Fraser couldn't bring himself to respond. Being in this house again after so long made him feel strange. The sound of the fridge opening brought Fraser out of his brief stupor and he dragged himself to the kitchen.

"Andrew forgot to go grocery shopping I see," Aunt Kimberly mutters.

The state of the kitchen took him aback. Dirt caked the tile floors, the dining room table was not only missing chairs, but unable to be seen under the pile of papers and envelopes. The kitchen counter was even worse, dishes, silverware, pots and pans spilling from the sink almost tipping to the floors. It reminded him of those shows where people were hired to clean homes where filthy was a minor way to put it. Whose kitchen did this belong to? It couldn't belong to his father, who was a well-known clean freak.

"What happened?" Fraser couldn't tear his eyes from the bizarre state of the kitchen. Aunt Kimberly shook her head and ran a hand through her hair, twirling the ends of her hair.

"Your dad just got a lot on his plate," she explained.

His father was never too busy to clean, he never would've let it get this bad.

"What-"

Aunt Kimberly's phone rang, she gave him an apologetic look before answering. "Hello?"

She paused, letting the person on the other end chat until their heart content, letting off a few sympathetic noises here and there.

"No, I don't mind at all, I'll be over there in a jiffy."

She hung up the phone and held out the house key.

"I'm sorry honey I gotta go, one of the mothers is in hysterics, so I gotta calm her down and take the kids. Why don't you take the keys and go grocery shopping?"

Fraser took the key to the house and Aunt Kimberly went and took another set of keys off the hook, tossing them to him.

"You can take the car in the back."

The back?

Aunt Kimberly was about to leave when she abruptly turned around and reached into her purse, pulling out her wallet.

"Here, use this to get groceries." She handed him a credit card. "You don't have to worry about the amount. Just make sure you at least have enough food to last you a week."

Fraser gave a slow nod, trying to process everything. Kimberly gave him an understanding smile and lifted on her tiptoes to kiss him on the cheek.

"Don't speed through the town; I don't need your dad lecturing me about how I've let my 'bad habits' rub off on you."

He gave her another nod, and this time Aunt Kimberly ran out the door without looking back. Fraser looked down at the keys and card in his hand, before shoving them in his pocket and tread towards the back of the house.

Opening the front door, Fraser saw dead grass everywhere, a dying tree and a shed, everything except a car. Was his aunt going crazy? Just for the fun of it, Fraser pressed the lock button on the keys, expecting nothing. A car beeped and he jumped. Confused, he pressed it again, and again a car beeped. He stepped down the porch steps and followed where he thought the sound came from. As he neared the forest that cut the town off from the outside world, he saw a silver Toyota parked in what looked like the beginning of a worn-down path.

It turned out his aunt wasn't crazy, but why was there a car and a path behind his house? It was giving off sketchy killer vibes and if memory serves him right, there was never such a thing. Though he never had the courage to even go near the woods, television shows and movies were right to always have crime scenes take place in the woods. The voices that would come from them had been the reason it took so long for Fraser to be potty trained.

He looked at the path that seemed to go deep into the woods. Maybe at the end of the path, there would be a log cabin that housed a crazy ax murderer or a beautiful woman that would ask to serve him tea before poisoning him and burying him under the floorboards.

Fraser unlocked the car, cautious to get in, his eyes flickering between the woods and the backseat of his car. His aunt might not be crazy but other people are and he didn't need anything to happen when he just got to town. Knowing the people of the town however, they wouldn't think twice about starting something with him. They couldn't stand oddity and if they knew he was back they'd have something to say. Goosebumps appeared on his arms and he took a thorough search of the car one more time.

Body still tensed up, he decided there wasn't anyone waiting to jump out at him from the woods or the back seat and started the car. It sputtered to life, and it made Fraser wonder if it was the car itself that he should be wary of. Paranoia at its finest. Fraser looked through the rearview mirror to see if he could reverse his way around the house without taking the side of it with him. Seeing no way around it, he tightened his grip on the steering wheel and put the car in drive.

The car moved at a snail's pace, a person walking by would easily pass him, but Fraser's vivid imagination wouldn't allow him to go any faster as he followed the mysterious path into the forest.

Did he and his father really need groceries? Couldn't they just wait until their aunt finished babysitting and take whatever food she conveniently made for 4 people? His parents couldn't cook for their lives and consequently, Fraser grew up eating his aunt's food. It wasn't always the best, her black hotdogs could attest to that, but that was the best option other than fast food.

Sighing, he realized he couldn't ask his aunt for food and he was sure as hell couldn't try and order fast food. As far as he knew no one in town knew he was here, and he wanted to keep it that way.

Fraser continued at a crawl, observing the trees that looked daunting even in broad daylight. It reminded him of a story his dad scared him with when he was a kid. Back when the town was first established, children would play pretend and hide and seek in the woods. It was fine until children who entered the woods would turn up missing and the town council had banned children from going into the woods. Police and townspeople searched every inch of the woods but there wasn't a trace that the kids were ever there in the first place.

Each generation told their kids that story editing and twisting the story to fit their need to scare their kids from the woods. Fraser kept flicking his faze left and right at the trees as if they would swoop down and snatch him from the car. He pressed his foot down on the gas pedal, hands tight on the stealing wheel.

What most generations left out, however, was that the parents of the lost children were so desperate to figure out how their children disappeared that they kidnapped the rest of the town's children and went into the woods. Both the children and the parents vanished.

The hairs on the back of his neck rose as fingertips brushed against him. Fraser almost crashed. As if the woods took pity on him an exit opened up and he sped out of the woods.

He pulled out onto the road, looking left and right for oncoming cars, surprised to see the sign; Welcome to Solidsville. The trail led to just outside of town. Since when? Having made the decision not to add another thing to think about, Fraser brushed it off as just another thing he forgot about from his childhood and drove back into town hoping to find the grocery store before nightfall.

Even though the town is small, Fraser still managed to get lost. He saw every little neighborhood and every tiny shop, everything except the grocery store. Only he could get lost in the place where he was born and raised for 9 years.

In frustration, Fraser made an abrupt turn before he realized he wasn't supposed to make a turn. He let out several expletives before randomly parking and laid his head back on the headrest, closing his eyes. His aunt asked him to do one thing and yet it was so difficult. His hands were shaking. He stretched them out and cautiously placed them on the wheel. Fraser let out a heavy sigh and opened his eyes one by one, then blinked. He made it. The bright sign *Solidville's Grocery* was hung up high for the whole world to see. After what felt like hours, he finally made it to the grocery store. If he had spent any longer looking for the grocery store, he might've cried.

His phone buzzed and he pulled it out from his pocket. It was a text message from his aunt.

How's grocery shopping?

If she was a mother Fraser would have tacked it up to mother's tuition.

Turning off the car he opened the door and almost fell out with his urgency. He forgot to lock the car and check to see if he had the card his aunt gave him on his rush to the grocery store. Had he been any more eager, he might've missed it getting colder outside or the awful stench that seemed to merge with the air. Fraser wrinkled his nose and wrapped his arms around himself vouching to rush inside and hope the grocery store would have some sort of warmth to offer.

It didn't…it was even colder than outside, goosebumps climbed up his arms and down his legs, his shoulders shook. He really should've brought a jacket, instead, he packed not one long sleeve shirt underestimating the weather and overestimating his ability to handle the cold.

"Hi, welcome to–"

Fraser looked up to the sales associate greeting him, dumbfounded at the look of disgust on her upturned face. Did he have something on his face? He gave a nod of greeting to the women and bound down a random aisle, feeling the associate's stare following him. When he could no longer feel the gaze of the sales associate melting the ice frosting on his back, he began to think about just what to buy for him and his father to eat. What does his father even like to eat? Fraser racked his brain but couldn't figure out what it was that his father liked or disliked eating.

He decided to get something easy to prepare so neither of them would burn down the house. Usually, if parents can't cook then magically the child learns how to cook, but that isn't Fraser's case, but he did try. He tried to do simple dishes like spaghetti for dinner or eggs and bacon for breakfast.. Nonetheless it all turned out to be disasters: the spaghetti sauce being burned with a nasty aftertaste and the eggs tasting like rubber, turned out to be food poisoning.

He looked at the frozen foods, eyeing the pizzas, and grabbed both the cheese and pepperoni pizza, the cold seeping into his already chilled arms. He should've grabbed a basket. Fraser turned around to look at the other options when he bumped into someone. Backing up he strained his neck to look at the man and nodded in apologies.
"Sorry I wasn't watching where I was going."
The man's lips twitched before it widened into a smile that bordered on predatory. "I see you're back."

Fraser's brows furrowed in confusion and took a closer look at the man when it dawned on him.
"Liam," he asked incredulously.
Liam ignored Fraser's realization and in turn walked a slow circle around him.

"You look the same as ever."

Fraser blinked, once, twice.

"Thanks?" He doesn't know whether to take it as a compliment or an insult.

"You know," Liam began in a matter-of-fact way. "It's interesting that you chose to come now of all times."

Fraser couldn't get over the fog of confusion surrounding his brain.

"What?"

Liam stopped in front of him and turned his head to the side and tapped his own ear.

"Is your hearing aid on," he asked. "Can you hear?"

Fraser's grip on the pizza boxes tightened, the cold starting to make his arms numb. He stared at Liam. The smile on his friend's face made him sick.

"Do you need me to repeat myself?"

He could feel his mind reeling back to the days kids in his class would ask him that question. It was like having a hearing aid was so different that people wouldn't let him forget it. Liam struck a nerve and he knew it. Gulping down the salt rubbed in his wounds he put the pizza back in the nearest freezer and turned around leaving the store. Unconsciously, he combed his fingers through his hair and arranged it over his ears.

Liam knew he was sensitive about his hearing aids, how much he was bullied growing up, and how many times his parents had to buy hearing aids because kids would 'accidentally' break them. Why would Liam tease him like that? How could he–?

A putrid smell assaults his nose, the strength of the stench stopped him in his tracks. "What is that smell?"

Against his better judgment Fraser followed the smell to the back of the grocery store revealing…trash cans. Trashcans? How could trash cans create such an awful smell, did they leave it there last year?

Fraser shook his head and turned to go back to his car, ready to throw the whole day away when he caught something in the corner of his eye.

A voice of reason told him to keep going, to go back in his car and go home. Yet he found himself turning around. Peripheral vision was tricky, it made you see weird things that made you do a double-take and realize it was just your imagination. It wasn't hand behind a trashcan it was plastic, the one they used to make life sized dolls.

Sweat beaded on his brow as bit by bit he inched closer to the trash can. Maybe it was a fake prosthetic or a part of a manikin that someone had disposed of and didn't bother putting it in the trash can. Ideas swarm his mind to dispel what his brain had already concluded as tears blurred his vision and fell down his cheeks.

He walked behind the trashcan and couldn't hold back the shriek that made his throat raw. Eyes void of life reflected Fraser as he felt the ground come from underneath him.

II

In the movies whenever a traumatic event happens, time always seemed to slow down until the person came to terms with whatever had happened. However, time waited for no one, Fraser included.

By the time Fraser dialed 911, all the cop cars that the small town could afford surrounded him and the scene and before he knew it a meaty cop handcuffed him and shoved him into the back of a car. It left him to analyze the day's actions over and over while the cops inspected the crime scene.

"I've never seen you before."

Fraser almost didn't hear him; the image of the girl was like cotton in his ears. He moved his gaze to the meaty cop sitting in the passenger seat, glaring at him with untrusting eyes. When did he even get in the car?

Fraser ignored the cop in the car with him and focused on the cops that were securing the scene, two men carrying a body bag that was heartbreakingly small. Where's the ambulance?

"Hey."

A glance was all he spared the cop trying to get his attention.

"Whose kid, are you?"

The bag was put in the back of a large car and the

cops slowly went back to their respective vehicles, their faces looked disheartened and more than one glanced angrily at the car that held Fraser in the backseat. It caused Fraser to stop replaying the scene repeatedly in his head and connect the dots, putting him in the back of a cop car, the glares, the questions. They think he did it.

The driver's door opened, causing Fraser to flinch and come back to the questions being shot at him. A particularly thin cop glanced at Fraser before easing himself into the driver's seat groaning, which seemed to make the passage easier. Once he had settled in, he patted his partner's shoulder and started the car.

"Has he said anything," he asked his partner quietly, just barely enough for Fraser to hear. The partner in question glared at him, his cheeks turned red as he shook his head.

"Haven't heard a peep from em'."

The cop in the driver's seat let out a heavy sigh and put the wheel in drive, pulling out from the back lot and making his way to the police station no doubt.

"My name is Henry," the cop announced.

It hurt Fraser's ears to have to strain them, Henry's voice was nearly carried away by the engine.

The cop continued as if he was talking to a friend, "I am chief of police. Might I know your name?"

"Fraser."

What harm could there be in telling them something many have forgotten?

"You got a last name," Chief Henry asked.

He thought about it for a moment before saying, "Bates."

Chief Henry rolled over the name in his mind to gain familiarity.

"I ain't ever heard of no Bates," the cop from the passenger seat announced. "Where you from?"

"Relax Hopper." Chief Henry clapped the cop on the shoulder.

Hopper forced himself to take a deep breath and let it out slowly as Chief Henry parked in front of the police station.

How long was the car ride, Fraser wondered. It couldn't have been more than 5 minutes. Not only that but how come it seemed like they were playing good cop bad cop? Were they trying to confuse him enough to give a false confession or was this really their personality?

Henry cut off the car and slowly got out bit by bit while Hopper jumped out, opened the door, and yanked Fraser from the backseat in the same breath.

"Careful with him, Hopper."

Chief Henry's words were put into motion as Hopper escorted Fraser into the hole-in-the-wall police station, however, as soon as they were out of Chief Henry's sight his words were void. Hopper dragged Fraser through the station that seemed to get the most of the town's expenses with its nice quality carpet and high-quality paint job and into a room where he roughly shoved him into a chair. Satisfied by his rough handling, he gave Fraser a devious smile and glided out of the room.

Silence once again became his companion and Fraser laid his head down on the table in front of him. He sat like that for a few moments, when the sound of a door opening ruined the silence Fraser was just beginning to welcome.

He picked his head up and watched Chief Henry enter the room and carefully slide into a chair opposite of him. Fraser noted the mirror behind Chief Henry, no doubt a two-way mirror. How many cops were behind there? How many had already convicted him in their minds?

"Fraser Bates," Chief Henry started slowly, having taken the time to sound out each syllable. It made Fraser uncomfortable.

He ignored Chief Henry and glued his gaze to the mirror hoping to make contact with one of the people behind the mirror and make them as uncomfortable as they made him.

"What made you come to this town son?"

I'm not your son, Fraser thought. And it's none of your business.

"Nothing."

Chief Henry let out a breath and ran a shaky hand through his thin hair.

"Alright," he began. "Since we've gotten to know each other, how about you tell me how you found the girl."

Fraser thought about not answering, before remembering he's a suspect. If he didn't answer he could get convicted.

"I followed the smell."

Chief Henry leaned forward; brows furrowed.

"What smell?"

Fraser's gaze was glued to the mirror when he forced himself to look at Chief Henry, studying his features. He genuinely seemed confused.

"What do you mean, 'what smell?'"

The stench was enough to make his eyes water. Was the man so old that he couldn't smell? But he didn't look old, the opposite, in fact, he looked young but weary of life. Chief Henry stared him down and studied Fraser as he did him.

"Son…there was no smell there besides the trash and that was fresh. The body too was fresh, there was no decomposing, there's no way you could smell the body."

"…Fresh?"

Chief Henry seemed to realize how that sounded and cleared his throat.

"She was just murdered, couldn't have been dead for more than 24 hours."

Fraser shook his head; the image of the girl scaring itself into his brain.

"Walk me through today's events," Henry suggested, leaning back in his seat but still on guard.

Fraser forced himself to relax and blank his face of any emotions as he too leaned back in his chair and forced his gaze back to the mirror, ignoring the cold that seemed to creep upon him.

"It wasn't me," he said. "I just arrived here this morning, my aunt took me home and asked me to get some groceries while she was taking care of someone's kids. I left the store and found…her."

Fraser didn't know how to refer to a dead girl but was sure it ought to be respectful.

"Your aunt?"

He nodded.

"Who's your aunt? What's her name?"

Hesitation from him had Chief Henry raising a brow. Fraser tensed automatically then forced himself to relax.

"Aunt Kimberly."

Chief Henry's brows raised, and his mouth fell open the slightest bit.

"Kimberly Wells, that works at the school? That Kimberly?"

Fraser shrugged.

"If there's another Kimberly Wells in this town I wouldn't know."

Chief Henry turned towards the mirror and gave it a meaningful look before he turned his attention back to Fraser. He studied Fraser for a moment before something else seemed to dawn on him.

"You Andrew's son?"

Fraser was hesitant to confirm it, however, he nodded, nevertheless.

"So, you're him, huh?"

A shiver passed through Fraser; the room seemed to get colder. It was only a glance that he took from the mirror to look at Chief Henry and that was all he needed. The man's eyes had hardened into a fierce glare, and he leaned away from him like he was diseased. He remembered Fraser. No doubt that those behind the glass remembered him as well and he was certain that soon everyone in town would know too. Not only that but him finding a body on his first day back…boy did he know how to rouse trouble.

The chill in the room seemed to soak into his clothing, Fraser repressed several shivers as he rubbed his hands up and down his arms slowly.

His phone beeped and instinctively he knew it was his aunt. Fraser wished she would appear and take him away.

The events of today began to sink in slowly, like a knife going through cold butter. He found a dead body, not just a dead body but a dead girl's body, a child that couldn't have been older than 5. Her body was so small, skeletal, curled up almost like she was sleeping on her bed, and wasn't dead behind a trash can. Never in his 18 years did Fraser think he'd see the dead, not in real life. Ever since he moved away from the wretched town the voices of the dead became that of a rarity, and he took that chance to stop associating himself with death in general. He didn't go to funerals or hospitals and if he could help it he didn't even watch death on television or read about it in books.

Fraser rubbed his hands vigorously up and down his arms as the cold had reached past his clothes and seemed to combine itself with his very being. Shivers racked his body.

Her hair was braided up nicely and prettily not a strand out of place. It was braided with ribbons. She even had pajamas on, pink bunny pajamas, not a speck of trash on her. Her skin was clean as she had just taken a bath before she was supposed to go to bed. But she couldn't make it to bed, death got her instead.

The cold froze his lungs, air became foreign to them, and he began to hyperventilate.

Her life had been extinguished before she could live it.

A hand pushed his head between his legs as his lungs felt like they were gonna explode.

"Breathe, son, breathe!"

The cold abated, his lungs thawed as Fraser gasped for air that now seemed to overwhelm him as he struggled to properly breathe, not knowing when to breathe in or breathe out or if he could.

The door to the room slammed open and a new cop said, "Miss Kimberly and Mr. Andrew are here."

Without a second thought, Fraser jumped up out of the chair, the chair flew back and clattered against the floor. He caused Chief Henry to stumble back and grab the table for balance.

"Where's my nephew!?"

Aunt Kimberly's voice could be heard by a deaf man.

"Fraser," his aunt hollered.

Fraser was in such a rush to move, to do something, anything that he tripped over his own feet and crashed to the ground. He scraped his hands against the concrete floor trying to grab something, anything to keep the world from spinning.

"Fraser."

His aunt sounded much closer now and when he looked up, there she was standing in the doorway, her face flushed red and her hair a tangled mess.

The moment she saw him, Aunt Kimberly sank to the floor and wrapped her arms around him. His hands twitched to push her off at the same time he rubbed his cheek against her, encouraging her comfort. It seemed like his brain was malfunctioning.

"Chief Henry," his father greeted as he walked over, ignoring his sister and son that was a pile of the floor, vouching to take the Chief in a handshake.

"Andrew." Chief Henry shook Andrew's hand in a firm grip. "It's good to see you, I just wish it was under better circumstances."

Andrew nodded his agreement and pushed his hands in his pockets, rocking back on his heels and looking everywhere but at Fraser.

"I heard from Debby at the registrar that she saw a bunch of cops surrounding the back of the grocery store and a young man being shoved in a police car. It's all over town that a stranger has been arrested and we all know the only reason why he would be arrested."

Chief Henry and Andrew shared a look.

Chief Henry cleared his throat.

"Well," the Chief began. "As far as we're concerned, he's just a suspect, I didn't know he was your son or Miss Kimberly's nephew. If I had known, I would've called you first."

The grip around Fraser tightened to the point he thought he would combust and he finally got the courage to gently push her away. Her grip tightened before she gradually loosened her grip however, she didn't let Fraser go.

"Chief Henry," she said with a fierce glare. "You took my nephew on what suspicion?"

He looked at her and his shoulders drooped.

"Well, he's the one who called the police."

Aunt Kimberly narrowed her eyes at him.

"If he called the police, why is he a suspect," she demanded. "Who reports their own crime?"

Chief Henry scratched the back of his neck but didn't look away from her. "There are killers who have done such things."

"Wha– this isn't Criminal Minds Chief Henry," she stated. "My nephew was traumatized by seeing a murdered child after he just got through an ordeal and came to us for comfort."

Fraser who was still cradled to his aunt's chest flinched. He was thankful his aunt didn't reveal his mother's death but to call it an ordeal….

"Haven't there been other townsfolk that have reported something suspicious," she asked. "Have you suspected them as well?"

Chief Henry stayed quiet.

The room was filled with silence so loud it hurt his ears. It was his father who broke it. Andrew cleared his throat and turned towards his sister.

"That's enough Kim," he said. "Chief Henry made a mistake, no need to hassle him. Now let go of that poor boy and let's get out of here. Wish you well Henry."

With that, he walked out the door and Fraser willed himself to look at his father. He was astonished by what he saw. His father looked as if he had just turned 60 instead of 40.

Wrinkles were his new identity, and his hair was more silver than brown. The subtle stubble that he said would never grow longer, turned into a beard and his hair brushes the tips of his chin, all greased up and in a ponytail. His clothes that he took pride and time in were baggy and wrinkled as if he slept in them. In front of him wasn't his dad, it was a stranger. Who was this man in front of him?

Kimberly let Fraser go momentarily for him to get up on shaky legs before grabbing his hand and pulling him out of there but before saying back, "Good day Chief Henry."

Although the situation was poor for it, Fraser wanted to laugh. Even upset, his aunt never forgot her manners.

They made it outside within a matter of seconds and Fraser was ashamed by how winded he was compared to his aunt who was just fine.

Andrew stood by his car and not making any sort of eye contact. It wasn't like Fraser wanted to have a conversation with him in the parking lot of a police station but to be avoided so obviously. He tried not to rub a hand over his chest.

Aunt Kimberly dragged him to the car and opened the door for him.

"I should be the one opening for you," he muttered unconsciously.

"Well, aren't you the gentlemen," his aunt quipped, rolling her eyes and walking away to her side of the car, getting in the driver's seat.

When she was all bucked in, she glanced at her brother and rolled down Fraser's window leaning forward the slightest bit.

Before she could say anything, her brother spoke first.

"I'm going to tidy the place up."

Aunt Kimberly balked before she conveyed her understanding with a nod and rolled Fraser's window up. They were silent as they watched Fraser's dad get in the car and drive off.

Once the car was out of sight Aunt Kimberly started her car but didn't drive off yet.

Fraser nodded and they too pulled out of the police station and made their way home. "It's been a while since we had a sleepover, huh?"

All Fraser could do was nod. Thousands of questions swam around in his head, making his brain hurt and his lips tremble. He kept nodding as he looked out the window and his aunt put a hand on his knee. A comforting notion that almost made him recoil.

As if it wasn't hard enough to come back to town,

he now has to deal with a murder and figure out what the hell happened to his father. Fucking fantastic.

III

He's grown, the spitting image of his father, not a hint of his mother in him. A pity since his mother went through life and death to make sure that child was born. No, he didn't look just like his father. If you look closely you can see the beauty marks he has, the faint freckles that decorated his face, like an image that was printed when there was only a little ink left.

In the end she died when he was 18 years old when he barely reached adulthood. There was no money left behind or anything for him to inherit so she left him with nothing. She abandoned him, it was ironic. She fought so hard for him to leave town knowing the horrors that awaited him only to leave him with the horror that is life, all by himself.

Fraser's ability is a crazy one no doubt, after all he found the body that wasn't meant to be found. He found her when her hair wasn't done. It wasn't curled the right way, it was supposed to be in pigtails, they would've looked cuter on her. Absolutely adorable. She was supposed to have on her slippers, so her socks wouldn't get dirty. Her makeup was also supposed to be done before she was found.

Charlotte was her name, a quiet girl who deserved better parents and a better birthplace than this town.

Everyone knew Charlotte was taken. The parents

were searching but the police knew she was dead. No one bothered to remember the days inbetween, when the kids were laughing forever silent, except the police.

They however, don't want the people to know and if they hadn't already known of Charlotte's body being found it would've been announced 3 days later, just like before. Poor Fraser, just can't seem to get a break.

IV

When Fraser was little, in the beginning of second grade, before he was able to get a hearing aid, his mom came up with a way to distract himself from the voices. Find a word, the first thing that popped into his head and speak out words that were similar.

Fast: speedy, quick, swift, rapid, unhesitatingly blistering.
Blistering: extremely fast, forcefull or impressive.
The townspeople were blisteringly fast.

Swift was the car ride home yesterday. Fraser was being mentally crushed by his questions while his aunt did his best not to intervene in his nephew's struggle. She didn't want to answer questions that she was sure would hurt him. Questions about what happened to his father. So, she pressed on the gas pedal and once they got to her house, they went their separate ways.

Fraser went to bed and woke up to the sun slipping in between his eyelids. He was planning on going back to sleep when the note that caught his eye dashed his plans. It was from his aunt:

Good morning Fraser,
I'll be out working so I won't be home until this afternoon. Go out and shop for some new clothes, use my card. I also got the car back so don't worry about

transportation. I'll be checking to see what you bought.
   Hugs and kisses,
    Your favorite Aunt.

She thought of everything. And not only that but…

You're my only aunt, Fraser thought as he rolled his eyes but couldn't help the small smile that made it onto his face.

Not wanting his aunt to come back home to a lump of disappointment still in bed, he rolled out of bed to do his business. He left all his stuff at his father's house so he couldn't take a shower as he didn't have a change of clothes. One thing he was going to do was brush his teeth, even though he didn't have a toothbrush. He found toothpaste in his aunt's bathroom and put toothpaste on his finger and brushed his teeth that way. The grimace made it difficult to brush his teeth, the experience itself was uncomfortable.

He tried to fix his hair so it wasn't a knotted mess but without a brush it wasn't going to work. Knowing his aunt would flip if he used her brush, since he gave her lice as a child, he used water to move most of his hair to cover his hearing aids. No one knew who he was and they were a dead giveaway.

He looked at his reflection. Dark circles surrounded his eyes and his skin looked deathly pale. He looked haunted.

Like the dead.

Fraser almost smacked his hearing aid out of his ear. Taking a deep breath he reached up and turned the volume up in his hearing aid. That voice. It was different from the one that welcomed him home or made that nasty comment at the police station. Something about it drew him in and scared him at the same time. He doesn't know whether it's because of the recent events or how much time had passed but the dead have become restless. They want to chatter his ear off, he can feel it.

Hearing that voice while actively having his hearing aids on scared him.

Deciding that ignoring the problem was the best solution, Fraser followed his aunt's instructions and went to go shopping. Her card was still snug in his pants pocket and the car was parked in the driveway. He was skeptical to step into the car just in case something happened over the period of time it was gone. The fact that his aunt drove it means she might've broken something from her manic driving.

He tested out the gears and checked to see if any lights were begging for his attention before deciding it was still safe to drive. His knowledge of the town was still a bit fuzzy but he settled on his brilliant idea to roam around town until he found a clothing store that fit his taste.

Luckily for him it didn't take long, there were only so many places where he could drive. The store itself blended in so well with all the other shops, all the buildings having the same faded color and wooden sign, Fraser almost missed it.

He found a parking space on the curb and did his best to parallel park without hitting the car in front of him. Had there been a car behind him he wouldn't have made it.

Satisfied with his parking he got out of the car and made his way to the little shop.

The bell chimed atop the door and Fraser suppressed an eyeroll. Such a typical thing for a small town clothing store to have.

"Welcome…"

In his mind, Fraser prepared for the people in town to be surprised as newcomers wasn't something that just happened. However, he didn't prepare himself to be given such an unwelcoming glare. Unwelcoming wasn't even the right word.

Menacing

Threaten: especially in a malignant or hostile

manner.

Perfect word to describe the look he had been given. He was tempted to step out of the shop and go home with his tail between his legs. Had Fraser not remembered that his aunt would be checking to see if he bought any clothes he would've been gone in the blink of an eye.

Instead, he forced his legs to move to the first rack near him. He was a medium in men's yet when he looked at the medium-sized shirts they seemed much too small. That and the deep-v neckline wasn't something he thought the men in the town would wear. He looked up to an XL but the shirts didn't look like they would fit right. Confused, Fraser looked around and scanned the store. The "Men's" sign hung on the other side of the room. He looked up where he was and saw the "Woman's" sign hanging proudly where he was standing.

In his haste to be busy under the harsh glare, he went through the women's section. He went through the racks of clothing, pretending to find them interesting, face flushed red. A look at the women behind the desk had him more scared than embarrassed when he finally inched his way to the male clothing on the other side of the store.

The shirts were more his style, plain and a crew neck. It didn't take him long to find his size either, he picked the colors out at random and when his arms were full of shirts he walked over to the front desk and gently set his clothes on the counter.

"I'm done," Fraser blurted.

The woman behind the desk, Dorothy, her name tag read, nodded, but otherwise stayed silent. He didn't miss the disgust on her face or the fact that she used her sleeves to grab the clothes and scan them. Fraser made a subtle glance at his hands to see if they had any dirt or he touched something that would ward Dorothy's actions. When he found nothing he couldn't help but stare at the women in disbelief. What was the problem?

Dorothy finished scanning Fraser's items and tapped the price on the screen. She wasn't even going to talk to him? Fraser wondered why she would take it this far. When he was younger the townspeople welcomed strangers with open arms. It was rare for someone to discover the town and would be embraced the moment they stepped out of their vehicles. So why was he being treated like this?

Fraser couldn't keep the obvious confusion off his face. Dorothy replied with a scowl and waited for him to pay. A headache came on and he no longer had the energy to figure out all the answers to his questions involving Dororthy. He paid for his shirts, surprised she even bothered to bag his clothes. She handed him the bag and his hand brushed her. Instantly, she pulled her arm back and he was more concerned than surprised. The force she used could've popped her shoulder out of her pocket.

He shook his head and stormed out of the store. People across the street were staring at him, with the same looks on their faces as Dorothy. It wasn't until he stared back that they kept moving, as if they weren't the ones looking in the first place. Frustrated, he threw himself in the car and threw the bag in the passenger seat. What is wrong with everyone? Fraser felt his headache getting worse by the minute.

He drove home, surprised to see his aunt's car in the driveway. She was home awfully early. A glance at the time on the dashboard let him know she was 3 hours early to be exact. If anything he expected his aunt to be late since she watched kids even hours after her job.

Fraser got out of the car, bag in hand, and slammed the door closed. There weren't any keys that were left behind for him to unlock the door. There needn't be any worry though, his aunt opened the door for him, but he'd rather be locked out. The scene before him made his chest hurt.

Aunt Kimberly stood in the doorway with eyes red and puffy with tear-stained cheeks.

"Wha…?" Words couldn't continue to flow from his mouth.

"I'm sorry," his aunt sniffled. "I didn't know."

Fraser was taken aback. Why was she apologizing?

"Aunt Kimberly let's go insi-"

"-Everybody knows," his aunt interrupted.

He blinked. What could people possibly know when hardly a day had passed. "Everyone knows that you've been arrested and so they blame you for the murder and…" Her words became nothing, but background noise. His ears were ringing.

It's your own fault
You found the body
It was only a matter of time
His ears continued to ring.

"-aser, Fraser…Fraser!"

He looked at his Aunt Kimber who was as pale as a ghost. A ghost…

The air was too cold. The glacial feeling consumed him as he blacked out.

V

It was so cold. Frigid. The air stood still, encasing Fraser until his muscles were frozen. His shoes were gone. He must've left them. He didn't remember the last time he had his shoes on, whenever he thought about it, the thought slipped away like a child running away from their parents thinking it's a game when they give chase.

The sky was dark, covered in shadow, he could scarcely count the fingers on his hands. It was like a cover on his eyes, he couldn't even see what he was standing on. Fraser's mind already recognized it was grass but he couldn't accept it. It was like thorns that dug into his feet, bruising them.

He needed to get out, he needed to get away from wherever he was, where the air held its breath and the silence was too loud.

Frost broke as Fraser lifted his leg up and stepped on shards of grass. The shadows moved and the clouds drew apart, showing the tiniest bit of light. His heart stopped. He didn't even know it was working until now. His blood had long turned glacial.

It was a gravestone, something engraved on it, but he couldn't see. So he knelt down letting the shards bruise his knees

The name on the gravestone...it confused him.

Charlotte Hampton
He didn't recognize it–

Not until a feather-like touch grazed his shoulder and blonde hair tickled his cheek. Fraser didn't want to turn around, he didn't even wanna exist at that moment. He squeezed his eyes shut hoping everything and everyone, him included, would just disappear. A hand brushed his shoulder and instinct escalated his fear.

No, no, no, no, no, no, no, no, NO.
It wasn't real, it couldn't be real.

Yet there she was. Walking right past him and up to her gravestone. In her pink bunny pajamas and lacy socks. Just like how he found her that afternoon. Her eyes were open this time. Brown eyes. They stared at him, the life long gone from them.

Charlotte Hampton, was her name. Fraser didn't know whether knowing her name made her death better or worse.

"I'm sorry."
He blurted out the apology before his mind could comprehend it.

"You're so young..."
His hair slid over his eyes, his body was so cold, it was shaking badly.

"You didn't even get to fully experience life."
The tears froze in his eyes before they could fall down his cheeks.

"I'm so, so sorry."
There was so much emotion in his voice.
Charlotte didn't say a word, just started aimlessly. She didn't look affected by the cold. She never would be.

Fraser's legs trembled so bad. He was kneeling on the ground but he felt like he was going to fall over. The grass crunched, it sounded like one was walking on gravel instead of grass. Frost chipped from his neck as he tilted his head up to watch Charlotte. She turned around and wordlessly looked behind her. Had the cold not frozen his lids he would've closed his eyes.

Had his eyes been closed maybe the sky wouldn't have opened.

Maybe the opening sky wouldn't have brought light to the other graves.

And maybe Fraser wouldn't have seen the kids standing next to them, wouldn't have had to hear their voices.

"Fraser."

"Fraser."

"Fraser."

It was like a hot bucket of water was thrown on him. He convulsed, trying to get air into his lungs, like a fish out of water. Instinct had him turning over to the side and stumbling out of his bed to the bathroom. He barely lifted the seat up before he vomited.

Bile burned his throat as loud, disgusting noises accompanied every heave. Even when there was nothing left, he continued to dry heave until his stomach ached and his mouth tasted like acid.

His knees throbbed as he forced his left to lift himself up and stumble his way to the sink. The faucet squeaked as he twisted the knob, releasing some warm water. He scooped water sloppily into his mouth and used the water to rinse off his face that felt like a block of ice. It stung with the clash of warm water and Fraser tried to squeeze his eyes shut but they were too cold, too heavy to move.

His legs shook as he continued to splash his face until he could blink his eyes sluggishly. A glance in the mirror and Fraser was horrified. His skin was so pale, as if there wasn't any blood flowing through his veins. Purple bruises surrounded his eyes that seemed to have sunken too far back in his skull.

"No," he whispered. "This isn't me."

His legs couldn't stand the burden and buckled. He smacked down to the floor, which sounded wet. Looking down he saw his clothes were soaked. He had left the sink on. It was overflowing. Fraser reached up, stretching himself impossibly thin and went to push the knob of the faucet, but it was already off. A look at the sink and there was no water. The floor was dry and so was he.

You're losing it.

Fraser shook his head over and over, his brain felt like it slammed against his skull with each shake. He wasn't losing it, he was just fine, he was just *tired.* It wasn't even daylight, the night must've been playing tricks on him. It always did.

He couldn't get up, his legs covered in goosebumps. Staying in the bathroom wasn't an option, it freaked him out that he still felt like he was submerged in water.

Crawling was the only thing that came to mind as he struggled on all fours to crawl to bed.

"Right arm, left leg, left arm, right leg."

His limbs twitched as his brain couldn't figure out how to move his limbs or which legs were his left and which was his right. Fraser had to whisper the mantra out loud to make sure he didn't fall. If he did he wouldn't make it to his bed, his safe haven. The nightmare and the shock he endured in the bathroom had exhaustion creeping on him, gripping his already tired limbs that were trying not to fold underneath him.

His light was on, if not he would've bumped head first into his bed, he gripped the sheet as he forced his legs to lift himself up. His muscles were crying, so taunt they were on the point of spasming.

Right as he pumped that last bit of strength from his quivering legs, exhaustion took the energy out of his arms and he face-planted into the bed. His eyes closed and sleep took him. Had he been in his right mind he would've noticed his hearing aids were thrown under the bed or the blades of grass hidden at the end of his bed.

Last night was nothing but a bad dream. At least, that's what Fraser told himself. He lost his hearing aids, but for once it wasn't a problem. There were no voices. He guessed that after last night's nightmare they decided to let him off. Even the dead could feel pity.

Good thing is after tearing his room apart he found them under his bed and perfectly intact. At least one thing was going well for him. He found grass in the bed but Fraser's brain couldn't handle the possibility of the dream being real, so it found the next best thing. Logical explanation. The town was surrounded by forest and they didn't have a great maintenance so dirt and grass must've collected in his shoes while he flopped around in them. When he took off his shoes and got into bed it must've come off his feet since Fraser doesn't wear socks.

That was it and yet the events that happened last night stuck to him like slime in one's hair. Only he couldn't cut it out.

However, his aunt was more than enough of a distraction. Yesterday his Aunt Kimberly went through a lot. Not only was she ridiculed at her job by those she considered friends but she was forced to leave her job. She said it was fine but the tears leftover on her cheeks said otherwise. While explaining what happened her voice kept cracking and faltering. He could tell she was holding her tears back until she finally excused herself saying there were leftovers in the fridge.

Dread washed over him thinking about what he would go downstairs to. Would his aunt be down there waiting for him? Would she still be on the verge of tears that made her eyes so glossy he could see his reflection? It broke his heart to see her go from being vibrant and passionate to being so…dispirited, as if life had been sucked out of her, but it was natural. If she wasn't teaching them she was babysitting them, if she wasn't babysitting them, she was finding new ways to make learning fun for them. Almost everything she did was for those kids and now she's not allowed to have any interaction with them. The kids were her life, she spent every waking moment with them. She was their teacher but to every kid she was another parent for them.

Fraser crept down the stairs, his head kept at a 90-degree turn hoping he'd be able to spot his aunt before his aunt spotted him. As much as he loved his Aunt Kimberly, he won't be able to handle her bursting into tears in front of him. He wouldn't know how to properly confront her and to do so would make him immensely uncomfortable. Forced contact and a display of unwanted emotion were not good separate, much less together.

One of the stairs creaked underneath him and every muscle in Fraser's body froze. He hadn't taken another step.

"Fraser," a voice rasped out.

His palms were sweaty and his head edge towards the sound. It was his Aunt Kimberly. She stood at the top of the stairs looking down at him, though that wasn't what frightened him, what caused alarm was the fact that she was still dressed in her pajamas and there was not an ounce of makeup. Her hair was a mess and she looked so tired. She'd been crying a lot, her eyes were overly red and puffy.

He couldn't speak as he looked at his aunt, his gaze repeatedly flicking up and down, spotting everything that was unlike her. His poor aunt.

"I wasn't able to make breakfast," she said softly.

Fraser shook his head too hard, it caused a headache. He adjusted his feet so he was turned towards his aunt and gave her a gentle smile, the action was foreign. It made his face feel too tight, his eyes too small.

"That's fine," he said. "I'm going to walk around

town for a while, then get us some dinner. Why don't you go lie down while I'm out?"

Aunt Kimberly's eyes looked so vacant.

He waited until she gave a nod of confirmation and turned around to walk back to her room. Fraser stood on the stairs until he heard the faint click of her door shutting before turning back around with a new sense of purpose.

Still in his clothes from two days ago and no shoes he grabbed the car keys and walked out the door. He jumped in his car and drove to the edge of town.

The edge of town is another saying for leaving town. It was used often in the old days but now it's a blocked off exit. The back exit is full of wild animals and there have been too many accidents. So they blocked it off and told the townsfolk and any unexpected tourists not to go through the woods near it. Now if one wanted to leave town they would have gone the way they came. Fraser however thought it would be the perfect place for a killer.

Along with the exit the schools were also pushed to the back of the town, so any activities they wanted to do like hold big events or just make as much noise as they wanted, there would have plenty of space and they wouldn't disturb the residents. In Fraser's mind that was reason number one that he kids have been snatched and no one blinked. There was another reason but it was one he wasn't yet willing to admit yet.

Ducking underneath a branch Fraser began to make his way through the woods. There were multiple worn down paths whether it was from animals or humans would be anyone's guess. He made the decision to get straight, it was the smartest way as the exit was the opposite way of the entrance. No circles or zigzags that would make him get lost and have to become the jungle boy. It wasn't until he stepped on a rock that he realized yet again he had no shoes on. It's like he was losing his mind.

Shaking his head he decided to look down at the forest floor to make sure he didn't step on any more rocks.

His neck began to cramp from how long he was looking down until he realized he was lost. There were no longer any various paths where you couldn't tell what species walked them. It was just fresh fallen leaves and sounds of birds tweeting here and there. Fraser wasn't even sure he was walking straight and his brilliant plan not to get lost, ended up in him being lost.

"O Christ," he muttered. "Way to go Fraser."

Looking left and right Fraser tried to distinguish his surroundings hoping he could magically find his way back. When he found he couldn't, Fraser let out a sigh and just kept walking forward. All he could do at this point was put one foot in front of the other, until he heard a child's scream. It pierced the air and made everything hush. He didn't realize that there were noises other than the birds until they stopped all together. Like they were holding their breath. More children were screaming and Fraser found himself running through the woods almost running into trees. The screams seemed to pierce his ears as he pushed his unathletic body into a sprint.

Giggle echoed through the woods and the sound seemed to come back again. The forest was no longer holding its breath. Fraser looked on to see an elementary school and its playground. There were tons of kids jumping around like they had no end of energy. They were screaming and laughing as they raced down the stairs and tried to be the highest on the swings.

Fraser panted with his hands on his knees ready to collapse. Never had he had to sprint like that in his entire life. He didn't even get to stretch first. One thing was for certain, someone couldn't snatch the kids with a high prison like fence surrounding the area. They had to take the kids some other way.

A dead end.

Someone tapped on his shoulders. Fraser spun around bewildered. There was no one there. Goosebumps appeared on his arms, he felt like he was thrust into a freezer.

Look down

Fraser snapped his head around. It was as if someone was talking directly in his ear.

Look. Down.

VI

The last thing he expected to find was a locket with a picture of his father staring back up at him.

It ended his day out before it even started. He stashed the locket in his pocket and was on auto-pilot when he miraculously found his way out the woods. The entire time his limbs moved stiff with fear that froze the blood crashing through his veins.

By the time he got in the car his teeth were chattering and the place where his shoulder was tapped felt like ice. It wasn't until he was at his aunt's house, locked up in his bedroom that he felt relatively warm…and alone.

Fraser sat at the foot of his bed and inspected the necklace. It was still dirty but if he cleaned it properly it would shine like it was freshly made, it was well taken care of. He turned it around and looked at the picture of his father. He couldn't be older than his early twenties, he looked so young. His hair was out of place and covered his eyes, he looked so fresh, so childlike, so…happy. Even as a child Fraser had never seen his father look so boyish and joyful.

A smile tugged at his lips as he carefully ran his thumb across the picture. It was a much better version of his father than Fraser had ever seen.

The smile fell from his lips. Why was the locket in

the woods? It was only a few feet away from the school. Whose was it? That was the most important question. Finding out the owner of the necklace might just be the easiest way to find the killer. Then his aunt could go back to what she loved and Fraser could stick it to the town. Naive thinking at its finest, the townspeople weren't as forgiving when he was younger and he doubted that changed now.

He looked out the window and saw it was getting dark. He needed to wake up earlier in the day, it was dinner time, even though he only woke up a few hours ago.

A look at his dirty clothes and disgusting feet had him clamoring into the bathroom and taking a hot shower to chase the bits of cold Fraser didn't even realize remained. Once he got out of the shower and looked at the time he realized dinner was on him. He forgot to bring back dinner. Groaning, he scrubbed his face with his hands. How could he forget?

In a small town like that one, there was no such thing as delivery and Fraser never drove around at night. It was a rule he and his mother had made long before he got his license. Aunt Kimberly must've been so disappointed.

Fraser dried himself off when he also realized that the only thing he bought in his hurry yesterday was a ton of shirts. No underwear, pants, or anything else that would let him walk around the house without flashing his aunt. He had to go shopping again and he needed to wash his only set of clothes so he could walk around town without getting arrested again.

He grabbed 3 shirts, the first one he pulled over his head and wore like a normal shirt, the second one he put his leg through the sleeve holes and put on as underwear wrapping the rest around his waist and tying it into a knot. The third one he used as a skirt in case his underwear unraveled. Not the greatest idea but it was better than being naked. Fraser grabbed his dirty clothes and placed it in a pile on the floor so he could get to it in the morning. No way would he stay up for the clothes to wash so he could put them in the dryer. He'd fall asleep mid wash and wake up to molded clothes instead of dry ones.

Aunt Kimberly hadn't texted him all day. If his aunt had a say she would text him every second everyday, but Fraser got her to do so once a day. Since yesterday there hasn't been no one single text. He needed to check up on her. The thought made his inside squeeze uncomfortably and as he left his room.

Fraser eased down the hall to his grandmother's room in a shirt skirt. Now that she was a ball of emotions she was also a ball of the unexpected. He doesn't know how to act around her, it's like walking on eggshells. His steps kept getting smaller until he was shuffling towards his aunt's door. He really didn't want to come to her room so late at night especially since he might walk into a crying fest. Love for a person could never be strong enough for Fraser to outright comfort them with no reservations.

He pressed his ear against the door to hear any signs of movement. There was nothing, no shuffling, breathing or signs of life in general.

Fraser hesitated before grasping the door handle. He held his breath. When there were still no noises coming from inside the room behind the door, he pushed it open wider. The door creaked loudly the rest of the way causing him to cringe and close his eyes. A few seconds went by when he opened his eyes one by one he opened his eyes and instantly relaxed at the sight of his aunt sleeping. With a bunch of curlers in her hair and drool that made a wet spot on her pillow. She was obviously cold gripping at the sheets underneath and the duvet that was slipping onto the floor.

He huffed and walked into her room, grabbing the duvet off the floor. Gently, he laid it across her and snuggly tucked it around her, especially her feet so she wouldn't have a chance at kicking the duvet off of her.

Satisfied with his imprisonment he eased back and carefully stretched.

"Andrew."

Fraser became a statue. Only his eyes moved as he looked down at his aunt. Her eyes were half open, unfocused. She wasn't looking at him. He didn't answer in fear of his Aunt Kimberly waking up completely. He'll wait for her to fall back asleep.

"It's happening again…the children. When do they get a break?"

Fraser's motionlessness was no longer due to the fear of waking her up. Oblivious of reality, his aunt kept talking.

"I'm tired of this town, Andrew. Maybe we would've left with Mary and Fraser."

Fraser doesn't know how long he stood frozen, his eyes pinned on his aunt. It took forever for the words to sink in, his brain trying to find the logic and his heart trying to reject the truth. His arms fell heavily to his side and he dragged himself from the room and closed the door softly behind him.

He stood in the hall for a few moments just outside her door. He wanted to go in there and wake his aunt up and demand answers. Fraser wanted to grab her by the shoulders and shake her. The thought was enough to make him stumble back to his room. He needed to calm down.

There were just too many questions once again and not enough answers. It made him question whether he would be able to answer them all. The answers that he does have are no help to him. Charlotte Hampton wasn't the first child to die. Nor will she be the last. There were no tourists in town except himself. Had there been he might not have been the only one arrested. That would mean that the killer was someone in town, which didn't help one bit, because no matter how cruel the townspeople could be, they were no killers.

Fraser sat on the bed and looked at the necklace hoping he would get something from the necklace he hadn't previously. Repeatedly he turned it over and over until the picture of his father began to blur. The need to find something, anything to make it seem like he had the answer to something became weaker and weaker until sleep won the war.

He should've set an alarm to wake himself up. By the time he opened his eyes it was well into the afternoon. His fingers were cramping from gripping the necklace tight during the night and his ear was throbbing.

Groaning, he forced himself out of bed and peeled the necklace from his hand, flexing it to take away the numbness. He needed a shower but he couldn't do so without clothes. Fraser flopped back on the bed and rolled himself back into the covers. He had to get up, but he really didn't want to. It would be so much easier to stay in his room all day.

"Come on Fraser," he muttered to himself. "You're already behind the day."

Fraser let out a sound of frustration as he jerked himself from under the covers and rolled out of bed. He hoped and prayed his aunt was still moping around in her room. He hated her feeling sad but he'd hate her seeing him like this more.

He looked at the space under his door hoping there would be a light. His aunt doesn't like wasting electricity, if it's on she was in her room still moping. If it wasn't he'd waste the day away in his room.

The light was on, Fraser did a mental happy dance and went to grab his clothes but touched the air. His clothes were gone. Where did they go? The clothes were funky but not so much that they'd get up and wash themselves. Did Fraser wash them last night and forget?

The door behind him creaked open. If he had common sense he would've ran back to his room but instead he stood there, staring at the spot where his clothes should've been.

"Good afternoon Fraser."

Shining as bright as the sun, his aunt came out, dressed fully head to toe. Her hair was out of rollers and made up of bouncy ringlets and her makeup, the usual overdone eyeshadow and off color blush were done..

"I love your outfit." She had the nerve to laugh. "I have your full outfit in the dryer downstairs. Why don't you go take a shower and I'll bring up your clothes. Hurry, I need you to run some errands."

She didn't have to tell him twice. He was out of her sight before she could blink. His face was red, he was so embarrassed. As much as he hated her seeing him like this, it was nice to hear her laugh. It was great to see her all dressed like usual.

Fraser was torn between staying in the shower long enough to let his embarrassment die down or to be quick like his aunt said. In the end he vouched for doing both, lasting more than 5 minutes but no more than 10. A medium shower.

When he got out his aunt had set his clothes on top of the bed like promised. Dressed in actual clothes was better than being dressed like a shirt-skirt.

He took a seat at the kitchen table and watched his aunt chop up some vegetables. "What are you making?"

Kimberly paused and looked down at the chopping block full of red onions and lettuce.

"I'm making your father some salad. He doesn't know how to cook, he'd starve if I didn't make him something."

He couldn't bring himself to order fast food, Fraser thought.

Even when her life was going to shambles she still thought about her brother. Fraser sighed in only child.

"Are you making him anything else," Fraser asked.
He wanted to keep the conversation going.

Aunt Kimberly shook her head and put the chopped onions and lettuce in a plastic bowl before adding some croutons.

"I already made him pasta and a few small meals that should last him for a week."
Fraser's brows touched his hairline. How long had his aunt been up?
"When did you start making everything?"
Aunt Kimberly shrugged.
"Since this morning."
He definitely needed to wake up earlier.
"Do you need help with anything?"

Aunt Kimberly nodded and added chopped up chicken to the bowl. "Can you take the food to your father for me?"
His face fell, this was not what Fraser wanted to help with. She put a lid on the bowl and added it to one of the many bags of food.
"Sure," Fraser grumbled. "Lemme get some stuff first."

Aunt Kimberly gave a smile of acknowledgement and he bounded upstairs to get his keys and wallet. He paused for a moment before grabbing the necklace off the bed and headed back downstairs to his aunt.

Looking at the huge bags of food, Fraser wondered if the food could make his father through winter. She's giving all that food to someone who didn't even call to ask if she was okay when Fraser knows for a fact his father heard about what happened with his sister.

Fraser played with the necklace in his pocket as she double and triple-checked to make sure everything she made was in the bags.

"Hey Aunt Kimberly," he began. "Do you know whose this is?"

She looked up from over checking the bags and set

her eyes on the necklace. He made sure it was closed, just in case she didn't know whose it was. Someone having a picture of her little brother around their neck might freak her out.

"It's your mother's necklace."

His mother's?

Kimberly pushed the bags of food towards him.

"Please have your father put the food in the fridge. I don't want my hard work to go bad," she droned.

With that, she left the kitchen and went upstairs to her room oblivious to leaving her nephew in a daze.

The necklace he found in the woods…was his mother's? That didn't make any sense. His mother wasn't the person to track the woods and lose her necklace by elementary school. His mother hasn't been here for years, and won't ever come back. Fraser tried to rub away his heartache.

His phone began to buzz and he pulled it out of his pocket. It was a message from his aunt, his father's address. Right. He had to take the food to his poor father so he didn't starve to death.

Sighing, he shoved the necklace and phone in his front pocket and grabbed the bags of food. His arms should've fallen out of their sockets with how heavy the bags were. Fraser set one down and hefted one to the car prior to doing the same with the other one. He made sure the bags were buckled up in the back seat. The last thing he needed was his aunt's love to spill out the containers.

He really didn't want to go talk to his father or even go near him. He didn't know how to react around him. Fraser's father kicked out him and his mother when he was younger but seeing him now…part of him pitied his father. He didn't like that. He wanted to stay angry because of what his father did to him, to his mother.

"Where are we going to go Andrew?" His mother clutched Fraser to her legs and he stared at his bare feet

wishing he was anywhere but here.

His father pushed Fraser's batman luggage towards him.

"Take this and help your mother with hers as well."

Fraser didn't move. He was counting how many different shades of brown were on the tile floors.

"Andrew, stop it!" His mother snapped, grabbing angrily at Fraser when he tried to run away. "We're not going anywhere."

It was as if his mother wasn't there. His father grabbed both his son and wife's luggage and set them outside.

"I'm not going to do this with you Jocelyn," he said coldly. "Either you leave or I make you leave."

The grip on his shoulders grew tight and Fraser couldn't count the varying shades of brown. Instead, he looked at his father who was so foreign to him. His warmth was gone, his eyes were steady and yet there was a darkness in them. It made him want to hide behind his mom, make her face those eyes that made his skin crawl.

His mother didn't want to face them either, because she grabbed Fraser's hand and yanked them from the house. This was the final argument they had. After screaming at each other day and night his father was no longer the nice guy and his mother lost her backbone. Andrew didn't even watch them leave. The moment they passed the doorway the door was slammed shut and locked behind them. Fraser pretended no to feel the tears wetting his hair, refusing to acknowledge the tiny sounds of grief that she failed to muffle. It was the first time he thought he would die of heartbreak.

The real heartbreak, however, is how Fraser didn't think much. He didn't think to use his phone as a GPS. Clicking on the address it redirected him to google maps and the realization of how much gas he wasted driving around aimlessly. He mentally cried as he pulled out the driveway.

The house was the same as when he first arrived only his feelings on mute unlike when he first stepped foot on the property.

Carrying the bags of food, Fraser channeled the Hulk and marched up the front door. Since his hands were full he kicked at the door as his way of knocking. The food was getting heavier by the second and he was seconds from falling over.

He listened to the sound of the door as sweat beaded on his forehead. The locks clicked open and soon he was face to face with his father. He looked better than Fraser had last seen him. His hair wasn't a greasy mess but a neatly combed ponytail and his prehistoric beard was gone, clean-shaven. If it wasn't for the lines decorating his face, a person would have mistaken him for much younger.

Andrew scratched the back of his head at the sight of his son and looked anxiously from left to right.

"What brings you by," he asked, crossing his arms over his chest.

It's a legitimate question. Why was he there? Anyone would want to know that question but for some reason it irked him.

He looked at the food then back at his father with a blank stare, he would've lifted up but it was all he could to make sure they were still in his grip.

Andrew made a sound of acknowledgement before awkwardly stepping back and opened the door wider. Fraser took a deep breath and set foot in the house. It still looked like it was going to fall apart but it looked… cleaner.

He went towards the kitchen and tried to ignore his father who followed him with an obnoxious distance.

The kitchen too had changed, the pile of dishes were gone and the counters were cleaned. It was as if the hoarder's mess was never there.

Fraser set the food on the kitchen counter and unraveled the bags. He took a container of food out and into the fridge that was concerningly empty.

"Do you mind next time," Andrew asked. "Like, calling me?"

He paused midway from putting a plate in the fridge. It took a minute for him to process the question. He also didn't want to admit how much it hurt that he'd have to call to enter his own house. Andrew took his son's silence for answer and eased himself into the kitchen using the table to separate them.

"Only because I might be doing something and it would be nice to have a heads up."

Fraser felt his expression turning sour. He set the food down and closed the fridge. Aunt Kimberly shouldn't have sent him here. He grabbed his phone and yanked it out his pocket.

Something clattered into the floor. Fraser and Andrew zoned in on the necklace. That wasn't supposed to happen.

"Why do you have that," his father asked flatly

Gone was the awkwardness, forced away by the seriousness of his expression. Andrew walked slowly towards it and Fraser felt the tension thicken the closer his father came to the necklace.

A familiar feeling of fear crept up his spine as his father bent down. He stared at it. It had fallen open and young Andrew was looking up at the older one.

"Why?" He stated. "Why do you have this?"

Fraser shrugged and tried to swallow back that seemed to be stuck in his throat.

"I just-," Fraser stuttered. "I just found it."

Andrew shook his head in denial, still staring at the necklace. Fraser eased himself away from his father

"Then you won't mind if I confiscate this."

Andrew picked up the necklace and watched it twist in the air. He looked dangerous. Fraser shook his head and took another step back.

"No, you can't. That's my mothers."

He watched as his father paused, then shook his head.

"That doesn't matter. I'm keeping it anyway."

The necklace had been enclosed in his father's fist. It shook as if his father were ready to swing on someone. His eyes, cold and dangerous, dared Fraser to say something. His eyes made Fraser want to run and never come back but he needed that necklace.

"You can't." Fraser's voice cracked. "I found it. I'm going to use it to-."

He felt his throat closing up. Andrew reared his head at his son, eyes going wide.

"Use it? To do what?"

Fraser couldn't speak, his mind was too busy focusing on suppressing the shivers that wanted to rack his body.

"I've heard it's not the first time there was a series of killings in this town, that it happened years ago as well."

His father's eyes narrowed, he looked absolutely predatory but Fraser couldn't stop talking.

"It's immoral, you all know it's someone in this town and yet you all let it happen. It's been hard on Aunt Kimberly, the town is isolating her. I'm going to help her. I need to help her."

Fraser's tongue doesn't cooperate for a moment and he chokes on his words.

"I'm going to solve the serial murders."

All the air had been sucked from the room. Not one since Fraser's babbling had his father moved. A statue would be jealous.

"Fraser…"

He called his name. All his father did was call his name, yet Fraser felt like it was a death sentence. He needed to plead his case.

"I-."

The backdoor slammed open and Liam walked in from the backyard, oblivious to the strangling atmosphere. In a flash his father altered himself. His body was relaxed and he stood awkwardly, a lopsided grin on his face.

"You finished the yard?"

Liam shook his head.

"I just need to plant a few things and it should be good as new."

Andrew nodded and gave Liam a soft smile. It made Fraser's heart hurt. His father never looked at Fraser like that.

"Thanks boy, I really appreciate it. Why don't you finish up and I'll get us something to eat."

Liam nodded in agreement.

Andrew grabbed his keys from the kitchen table and gave Fraser a lingering glance, his eyes never changed. It made Fraser flinch and Liam remained unaware.

The door clicked closed and Fraser slid down the kitchen wall he didn't realize he was using to stand up. From the tip of his toes to the top of his head he was covered in a cold sweat.

Liam walked over to Fraser, his heavy boots thumped against the hardwood floor. Each time they thud against the floor his heart jumped. He thought he was going to have a heart attack. Liam kneeled down next to Fraser and leaned forward.

He kept leaning forward until his lips brushed Fraser's ear.

"Fraser…"

His hearing aids blinked out, like a power outage.

Teller of Liessss

The hissing made his body shake.

Who was that?

His hearing aids recovered and he caught the last bit of what Liam was saying.

"...I can help you find the killer."

VII

It was too familiar for Fraser to think this was a dream.

The hospital room, the stench of cleaning products, the beep of the heart monitor, the all too bright light, the stale atmosphere, the air being let out of the doctor's rolling chair, the-

"What are you thinking so hard about?"

Her limp hair, washed out skin glistening with sweat and eyes that stayed more close than open. A body that lost all its muscles over time and was only skin over bone, sickness had taken almost every light out of her body. Almost. Her eyes shone, they were full of life even though death loomed over her. It killed him to look into them.

"Fraser?"

Her calling out his name snapped him out of his observations and looked up at her. Regret. He snapped his gaze back down to the poorly decorative tile.

"Sorry," he apologized. "I wasn't paying attention."

She kicked her feet as she struggled to get up. Fraser heard her struggles, but he curled his toes until his feet muscles spasmed, to stop himself from jumping up to help her. She hated being helped. Always did and always will, she told him. He thought that was ludicrous.

"What's gotcha thinking about so hard you lettin'

life fly by?"

Fraser shook his head and stared hard at the floor tracing the lines between tiles until it caused his vision to blur.

"O come on," she coughed. "I don't bite."

He sighed. She was never going to let him keep a thought for himself.

Fraser bit his lip and forced his shoulders to relax. It didn't matter what he told her, it would stay forever in his mind, his mother was dead and no matter how many times he tried to hear her voice from beyond he never succeeded.

"Mom," he began. "I found your necklace in the woods."

"Oh."

Fraser frowned. His mother wasn't one to give short answers.

"Mom I-"

"Do you know me, Fraser?"

He couldn't answer his mom. Even when alive she was a mystery, always giving riddles, throwing him into confusion.

"Look at me Fraser. Tell me you know me."

He shook his head. He wouldn't, couldn't look up at her. It was bad enough to dream of her on the exact day she died. Looking at her would set his heart aflame.

"Look at me Fraser."

It wasn't even his mother's voice. It was a class of children speaking all at one time, overlapping each other.

"LOOK AT ME!"

She grabbed his face and pulled it an inch away from hers. Her eyes were gone, swallowed by darkness.

"See those you've let die."

A scream from deep within erupted from him as his body vibrated with violent shivers.

"No," he cried out. "Nooo."

His bedroom door burst open as his aunt threw

herself into the room and to her nephew.

"Fraser, you're freezing wha-"

She spotted his hearing aids on the floor and dashed towards them before trying to put them back on Fraser. The poor boy was shaking so badly they would fall off every time she tried to secure them on his ears.

"Fraser please."

He couldn't hear a word she was saying. In fact he couldn't hear anything. Not her, or muffles or the voices of the dead, only silence. Fraser moaned in pain as he clawed at his ears trying to get rid of the awful silence.

"Fraser, stop." His aunt began to cry.

Her tears fell onto Fraser's face but he couldn't stop. He continued to scrape at his ears until layers of skin collected underneath his fingernails. Aunt Kimberly frantically grabbed at his hands while trying to keep a hold of his hearing aids.

"No Fraser," she begged. "Please be patient. I'll get them on, I promise. Just please…"

He didn't want to hear anything but he didn't want to not hear anything. All he wanted was peace but that was like hell not being hot.

"I need," she choked on her tears. "I need to get these hearing aids on you. I need to get you warmed up. I need to help you but how?"

Fraser continued to struggle as his aunt's tears rained down his face. He could feel his mind fracturing, his body was too hot and too cold. His ears were throbbing and the world was spinning. It felt as if the world was crumbling to the ground.

Aunt Kimberly tried again to put on his hearing aids but they were smacked out of her hands. They flew across the room out of sight.

"No Fraser-"

Wail. All he could do was wail. He couldn't hear it. He could feel it, his sadness coming out from his lungs but never leaving him. With each bit of sadness that leaves it returns, from the anguish, the pain, the *despair.*

Sobs racked Aunt Kimberly's body, she didn't know what to do. She tightened her embrace around him and rocked him back and forth, humming between the sobs that wounded her throat. Her hums vibrated through her chest and into Fraser's body.

Little by little her humming calmed him down until his wails turned into quiet whimpers. She continued to rock back and forth until their tears dried on their cheeks.

Aunt Kimberly wanted to get Fraser's hearing aids, but as soon as she attempted to detach herself from him, he would let out sounds of distress. With no other choice but to stick to him like glue, she eased them down to a lying position before pulling the covers up until it brushed his chin.

She continued to hum until her eyes began to droop, and sleep claimed its next victim, however Fraser refused to become one. His eyes remained wide open through the night, while humming to himself.

Throughout the night, every time he closed his eyes Fraser would force them open. He would blink rapidly in an effort to keep his eyes open. It was the only method he knew of. He heard blinking was like mini naps. It was a myth, a ridiculous one at that, but desperation knew no boundaries.

Aunt Kimberly stirred next to him and he closed his eyes pretending to sleep. He didn't have the courage to face his aunt. Fraser couldn't believe he had a meltdown in the middle of the night and if that wasn't bad enough he cried like a newborn baby. Shame burned his ear and cheeks and made his eyes water.

He felt her presence leave him when she got out of bed. Fraser's body began to relax, his muscles sore from tensing up all night. His aunt shuffled around and the warmness of the blanket slowly tried to lull him to sleep, he could feel it try to take him and Fraser wished his aunt would hurry up. He might not be able to hear her but he could feel her presence. He didn't want sleep to capture his mind after it already fractured it.

Will alone could only keep him awake for so long, Fraser tried to kick his legs sleepily but it was sluggish, sleep had already grasped his feet and legs, he slid his hand under her pillow and twitched his fingers one by one, counting them over and over. It was as if she would never leave.

His mind slowly shut itself down and sleep seemed inevitable when suddenly he felt alone. With a groan, he rolled out of bed. Barely standing up right he stumbled into the bathroom, throwing himself into the bathtub and hitting his head on the bathroom wall. Sleep still grabbed at him as he turned on the shower. Coldwater rained down on him and Fraser bit his lips, teeth sinking into flesh as he suppressed his scream.

A little too far, yet under no circumstance would he go back to sleep. That nightmare was too much for Fraser's mind, it tore open the fresh wound that had only been trickling blood but easy to ignore. Now it was gushing out and he could do nothing to stop it, he had no idea how to deal with it.

Fraser tilted his head back and let the cold water rain onto him. Never did he think his life would get so messed up. Yet at the same time, it's to be expected, his life had foretold itself as soon as his ability to hear the dead came to light. What was he doing with his life?

Are you lost?

That voice. It stood out in his nightmare, among the children. It was older, around his age. It made him wonder how she became a victim of death.

"What do you want," he asked the darkness.

What you want.

What Fraser wants…

"What do I want?"

Fear. It trickled down his body and mixed in with the water. His body became numb with it.

The truth.

He snorted. The truth, huh?

"And you know the truth?"

He does

"Who?"

The answer doesn't come.

Fraser turned off the shower head and laid in the tub. His only outfit was soaked to the point that it stuck to his every crevice. He breathed heavily out his nose.

No longer having the energy to care about such things he stripped out of his clothes. He'd dry them when his aunt was no longer downstairs, he didn't feel like putting on a shirt-skirt. Hell he didn't even feel like getting out of the tub. Still, he pulled himself out of the tub and trudged into his bedroom.

Fraser's phone beeped as he grabbed a dirty towel to dry himself off. He really needed to do laundry. Looking down at his phone, he gritted his teeth as he saw a message from Liam.

Be ready in 10

Fraser groaned and put his head in his hands. Great.

Liam came the exact time he said he did, too bad Fraser's close took longer than 10 minutes to dry. Aunt Kimberly waved at him through the front window, because she looked presentable. Hair done, make up flawless and dressed in an outfit that insinuates she went gardening. Fraser didn't want his aunt to invite a snake like Liam into the house, so he did the only thing he could do. Wear his aunt's clothing. He wore the most gender neutral top and bottoms that his aunt wore yet even a blind man could see he was wearing women's clothing.

When he got in the car, Liam's brows touched his hairline.

"Nice outfit."

Fraser couldn't look him in the face.

"Shut up, I need to go shopping."

Liam's smile fell.

"Let's get going," he said.

Fraser was starting to regret getting in the car with him. He inherited his aunt's speeding habits as he careened through town. He slipped his hand into the handle at the top of the car door and tried to stop himself from pressing down on the imaginary brake pedal.

"Relax Fraser, I'm driving the speed limit."
If the speed limit was 80 mph then he might've believed him.

"My aunt said this wasn't the first time," Fraser began casually. "The murders…"

He ended off more awkwardly than he intended, hoping a casual attitude wouldn't make the question as awful as it tasted in his mouth.

Liam didn't answer for a while. He took a deep breath and let it out slowly. "I'll answer you questions when we get to the shopping center."

He pushed his foot down on the gas pedal, and they arrived at their destination sooner than they should have. Liam parked haphazardly in front of a store and pointed to the clothing store next to them.

"We can shop for clothes here."

Liam got out of the car while Fraser sat there speechless. Liam's parking blocked half the already narrow street. He got out of the car and gestured widely to the bad parking.

"Someone would have to hit your car to get by."

He paid Fraser no mind and went into the clothing store.

"Liam!"

He followed Liam into the store and paused. It was almost empty. Dust surrounded every corner and if there wasn't a person sitting at the register on the other side of the store he might've considered it abandoned.

Liam picked up a pair of pants and put it around Fraser's neck. It didn't reach all the way around his neck and Liam folded it back up and threw it back down. He was using a mother's trick. Put the jeans around ones neck and if it goes all the way around it should fit ones waist. Fraser felt it unnecessary.

"Liam-"

"Relax Fraser," he sighed. "No one's coming down this road."

Fraser wasn't relaxing, his jaw kept clenching anxiously and his eyes didn't know where to look at. Liam grabbed another pair of pants and fit them around his neck. The pants overlapped each other a bit and Liam must've decided they were perfect because he threw them at him. Fraser fumbled the pair in his hands before properly catching them.

"Find a few more pairs and we'll see where we can find shirts as you can see the place is cleaned out of them."

Fraser was too tired to play along with Liam. He didn't go out with him today to just go shopping.

"You said you know the killer," Fraser reminded.

The lady at the register flinched but otherwise showed no other response. Liam glared at him and grabbed a few more pairs of pants before approaching the counter and pushing them to the lady.

Mindlessly she scanned the items, not even looking at the two of them. It was as if he was invisible. She rang them all up and Fraser groped for his wallet when Liam pulled out his card and swiped it.

"You didn't have to do that."

Liam rolled his eyes.

"A simple thank you would be nice."

"Thank you," Fraser said.

He said it was just not towards him. The woman

gave him the bag full of pants and Fraser gave her an awkward smile.

The lady looked at him and he took a step back. Her eyes…they looked just like Charlottes.

He was so shocked he didn't notice that he was staring until Liam dragged him outside.

"It's not polite to stare," Liam quipped.

Fraser couldn't get over her eyes.

"Was that her?"

Liam raised a brow in question.

"Was that her," Fraser repeated. "Charlotte's mom."

He shook his head.

"No, she's a victim."

Liam walked away leaving Fraser to struggle to catch up physically and metaphorically.

"What do you mean a victim?"

Liam went into another store, thats door was propped open, only this time it truly had been abandoned. There was no one at the register and the clothes were all covered in a layer of dust.

"Do you remember when we were kids, before you lost some of your hearing we used to play with these groups of kids?"

Fraser shook his head.

"Well in the group there was a pair of twins, James and Kaleb were their names. That was their mom."

He didn't like where this was going.

"They were the first ones to be murdered."

The women's eyes were that of the living dead. Alive but dead inside. Now he knew why.

"The murders started a few months before you left."

This was news.

"Then they stopped a week after you left. Now that

you're back the murders are happening again."

Fraser could feel his head spinning.

"Why didn't I know about the murders before I left?"

Liam had the audacity to laugh. A full body laugh to the point where he had to bend over to catch his breath.

"Seriously Fraser," he asked. "How could you? You were too preoccupied with your mom and dad fighting over poor little Fraser hearing a voice that nobody else could. Your parents shielded you from everything that could harm you."

That was an ignorant thing to say. Fraser had to leave town because people couldn't treat him like a normal person, isolating him and talking about him as if he wasn't a human being. Liam read Fraser's thoughts.

"I'm not saying you didn't have your trifles but you didn't notice kids disappearing. Kids cowering in fear and adults in tears because everyone was afraid that their child would be next. Even now, half the town is missing."

He gestured around the empty store.

"Half of the town is full of empty shops and homes because people were so scared they left. The ones left are those who have ancestors that they couldn't leave behind or are empty shells whose children had already become victims."

"Liam I came here to-"

"Solve the murders," Liam exploded. "Why?"

"Aunt Kimbery," he explained quietly. "If it wasn't for me coming back and finding the body they wouldn't have blamed her. I just want to help her be happy."

Liam chuckled.

"Fraser, are you dense? We know Kimberly and you aren't involved in the murders, but it's easier to blame a freak of nature and his aunt than to find the real killer hidden amongst friends and family."

Isn't Aunt Kimberly family?

"Fraser, why did you take up my offer," he asked. "To solve the murders. Your family love isn't so strong that you'd try to find a serial murderer, so why?"

He didn't know.

"At least I have a family."

That was a low blow. Even for Fraser. He could see it hurt Liam, even if he didn't want Fraser to see it. The pain in his eyes and the slight tremor of his lips. Fraser couldn't bring himself to apologize so without a word, Fraser turned around and walked home.

VIII

It's been 3 days since he and Liam parted. 3 days since Fraser's carried guilt around, 3 days since he's been able to go to sleep. The nightmare was too much for Fraser and every time he closed his eyes he saw the twin's mom and the dead look in her eyes. They followed him, throughout the day and throughout the night.

Aunt Kimberly had noticed yet she hadn't brought it up. She might've thought her quick glances of concern weren't obvious but they were. To make him tired she would send him out on errands, but when he looked at the townspeople, really looked at their faces he couldn't help but feel guilty. Liam was right. He wasn't aware of the world around him, of reality.

If he had been paying attention he would've noticed that all the kids weren't going to school. Those who did stuck to themselves and were even afraid of the teachers. How most of the parents kept to their homes afraid that their children would be the next victim.

The ones that didn't have children had no fear, instead they showed hatred. To Fraser and his aunt. Not once when he came back did he notice. The suspicious glances, the fear. All he was worried about was himself, while the town was living in hell. The killer was someone the townspeople trusted, someone everyone in town knew and grew up with. That in itself is devastating, having to look over your shoulder in your own home.

Aunt Kimberly saw the disheartened expression on his face every time he would get back from town and stopped forcing him to go out. Instead, she tried to have him busy around the house, hoping it would tire him out and cause him to sleep. She underestimated Fraser.

He'd take more cold showers lately. Fraser didn't know the last time he'd been warm. Even under layers of clothing his skin was like a sheet of ice, covering wintry bones. His daily routine was pretending sleep didn't exist. He was tempted to pretend as if nothing existed, reality was too cruel to handle.

If he had been paying attention he would've noticed that all the kids weren't going to school. That when they did they kept to themselves and were afraid to interact with students and adults alike. How those who didn't go to school would be locked inside their homes, their parents afraid they'd be the next victim.

The ones that didn't have children had hatred. Seeing the children scared of their own shadow made the hatred build to a point where it needed an outlet. With suspicion already pointed at them, what better reason to put the blame on Fraser and his Aunt.

All he was worried about was himself, while the town was living in hell. The killer was someone the townspeople trusted, someone everyone in town knew and grew up with. That in itself is devastating, having to look over your shoulder in your own home.

Aunt Kimberly saw the disheartened expression on his face every time he would get back from town and stopped forcing him to go out. Instead, she tried to have him busy around the house, hoping it would tire him out and cause him to sleep. She underestimated Fraser.

He'd take more cold showers lately. Fraser didn't know the last time he'd been warm. Even under layers of clothing his skin was like a sheet of ice covering wintry bones. His daily routine was pretending sleep didn't exist. He was tempted to pretend as if nothing existed, reality was too cruel to handle.

Fraser coughed and wiped his nose on his sleeve. He didn't know whether he was releasing snot or his nose was just that cold. He'll go with the latter. Something else to add to the shit show he called life. Fraser was ready to throw a pity party, though he'd had to solve the murder first. His aunt still wasn't allowed back at the school. She had gotten better by managing to dress herself everyday and look happy but Fraser had this nagging fear that she was going to fall back into a depressive state. Except this time, she wouldn't be able to pick herself back up.

A knock sounded on his door and Fraser sat up from the bed, his spine cracking in protest. He looked at the time, it barely reached the afternoon.

"Come in," he called.

The door twisted open with a quiet click and opened just enough for Aunt Kimberly to
pop her head in.

"Good morning Fraser," she chirped. "Did you have a nice sleep?"

Fraser didn't want to lie to her. He looked at the time once more.

"It's the afternoon now," he drawled blinking sluggishly

Aunt Kimberly huffed at the correction and opened the door wider, fully stepping into the room.

"Good afternoon," she amended. "Want some breakfast?"

Fraser didn't even feel like walking around his limbs felt heavy and his head hurt. "Yeah, I can eat a little."

She nodded and skipped out of the room on the way to make breakfast, but not without
closing the door first. Fraser had begged her to get into the habit of doing so, he didn't have to pretend behind closed doors.

He dropped back down on his pillow and let his head sink into the softness of the pillow. It was a relief for his head that felt as heavy as a bowling ball. It wasn't until the smell of bacon that Fraser realized that he smelled something else as well. Lifting up his armpit he gave it a few sniffs, recoiling at the smell of onions.

"Time to take a shower," he muttered to himself.

It would pass time and by the time he got out breakfast would be ready. Yes, taking a shower would be very beneficial.

He rolled onto his stomach and slid off the bed until he was forced to stand up straight. Fraser's muscle weakened and he stumbled. If it hurt more to fall he wouldn't have bothered to catch himself. He sneezed and wiped his nose with his sleeve. This time he was 100 percent certain that there was snot coming from his nose. A look at his sleeve told him he was right.

A cold shower was just what he needed to help his sore muscles and fragile bones. When
one was sick it seemed as if they had aged too many years. It was a feeling that made the sick
feel even sicker. Fraser just wanted to jump back into bed and let the day fly away.

Water dripped from Fraser as he stepped out of the bathroom. An idea had struck him in the shower and he wasn't sure if it was the sickness or the guilty conscience but he grabbed hisb phone and texted Liam.

I still need your help, meet up later?

Fraser was a mess. He still hadn't apologized and yet he was asking for his help. Real classy.

A knock at his bedroom door had Fraser hobbling over and putting his weight on it. He'd preferred if his aunt didn't see how deadly his frame looked. The door handle jiggled and his aunt tried to open the door.

"Breakfast is ready," she yelled, her voice muffled.

"I know," he said. "I'll be down in a moment."

He could hear her huff in annoyance and imagined the roll of her eyes and waited until he heard her retreat downstairs before getting dressed. His clothes didn't fit him like they were supposed to these days either they rubbed too much or the texture was different. It felt like his aunt switched his clothes. Maybe she did. If she did he wouldn't ask about it. It was too much work and Fraser already had enough on his plate.

The trip downstairs was taxing, the cold shower seemed to have the opposite effect on him than he wanted. His skin felt too tight and his muscles too large. Even his bones felt like they were too thin and they would snap.

Breakfast was a quick affair, Fraser didn't eat much and neither did Aunt Kimberly. She was distracted while Fraser genuinely didn't have an appetite. He didn't know whether the sickness or the lack of sleep took away his desire for food.

When Fraser could stomach no more he excused himself from breakfast and told his aunt he would be back. He couldn't wallow and rest in his bed all day, something was itching at his mind to get up and out of the house.

Fraser barely got the car started when he pulled out of the driveway. He didn't even know where to go. So it's no surprise that he ended back where he started. The beginning and the end of town, where they welcome and wave goodbye to residents and tourists alike, though it's more likely to be residents than tourists.

The last time he was in the forest he didn't use any

of the paths and got lost. He needed to
pay attention to even the smallest details and couldn't rule
anything out and the forest sometimes liked to keep secrets.

He slammed the car door and walked into the
woods. Fraser entered the forest and studied the paths
before choosing the most worn down.

Fraser lumbered in the woods paying attention to
everything else but the person in the woods.

When he finally saw the person he stood at a stand
still. He wondered if she should leave. His headache was
getting worse and Fraser's ears began to ring before his
hearing went out altogether. His hearing had the worst
timing.

The person hadn't noticed Fraser but he didn't
want to move in case he made a sound that would alert the
person he was watching only a few feet away.

Follow him

What?

Follow him

It was the children again. The voices were of
overlapping children. Was he dreaming again? When did he
fall asleep?

Move! Follow him.

Mindlessly he began to follow the person.

Don't...

It was the women from the bathroom. The one that
offered him the truth.

Don't follow...him.

No, follow him. Keep going.

Don't follow him.

No!

The voices clashed inside Fraser's head until his
eyes lost focus and his head throbbed in
pain. He tried to choke down his pain but couldn't hold
back his grunt. The person froze and so

did Fraser.

Shit, shit, shit.

The person started running and Fraser stumbled after him, the distance going from a foot to a mile. It was like a lucid dream. His hearing aids weren't working, everything was happening in silence, maybe this wasn't real.

The person jumped off the path and Fraser followed, going deeper into the forest. Fraser pumped his legs to go faster, adrenaline the only reason he made it thus far. He rapidly closed the gap and reached forward a breath away from him.

Fraser trips and lands face to face with eyes void of life. As if his life couldn't get
any worse.

Fraser screamed.

X

You'd think after the first body Fraser would learn his lesson. Though in his defense it's
not like he expected to see a second body. No one really expects to see a body, even if they're
investigating serial murders.

The moment the cops caught sight of him Fraser knew it was over. The policemen were
already tense but when their eyes landed on him, they turned downright hostile. It was like when a dog couldn't find their owner and when they finally did they saw them with someone else, someone they considered a threat.

Fraser couldn't pay too much attention to the police men though. His mind seemed to take in the details of the body without his consent.

It was a boy this time. He looked a little older than the girl, maybe 7 years old. He had
Fraser's brown hair and eyes were so dark they looked black. The boy wore a button down collared shirt and bermuda shorts. The killer didn't give him shoes to wear.

Since he called the police Fraser had been staring, studying every detail of the boy, his knees pulled up to his chest. The boy's skin was tanned yet so pale as if his skin couldn't bring itself to look alive. The boy was beautiful. Ordinary features transformed to gorgeous by long lashes, high cheekbones and full lips. If he had a chance to grow up he certainly would've been a looker. Maybe that's why he was a target.

"Get up."

Fraser looked up from his position to the cop, who looked more bite than bark. His tone was harsh but looked as if strong wind would hurt him.

"Now."

It took 20 minutes for the police to find them in the forest. During that time Fraser didn't move a muscle, he was too scared to blink, shaking like a leaf, hoping the clouds gathering in the sky would cry so he could wash his tears away.

Fraser sneezed. He didn't have the strength to cover his mouth and was glad none of his

snot got on the body. His face was awfully congested, he really needed to hurry up and get over

his cold or sooner or later he'd be in the morgue.

"Ah!"

He yelped as his arm was grabbed and he was yanked to his feet.

"I was getting up," he groaned.

The cop grabbing him, a different cop, looked mean, real mean, like he was ready to take a bite out of Fraser. He hoped the cop caught his cold, he almost pulled Fraser's arm out of his socket.

"Not fast enough," the cop sneered. "And you contaminated the crime scene."

Fraser cringed.

"Any evidence you wouldn't find it anyway," he tried. "You took forever to get here."

The cop looked ready to add Fraser's body to the crime scene. If eyes could kill...

"It took us a while to find you where you were," the cop gritted out. "We couldn't find you."

Fraser tilted his head and raised a brow.

"You really couldn't find me?"

The cop ground his teeth, Fraser was scared for his teeth and knew for a fact that his jaw ached.

"No," the cop clipped. "Get. In. The. Car."

Fraser doesn't know if it's because his brain is trying to grab onto the least important fact but he couldn't get past the fact that the cops wouldn't find where he was. Did they not follow the path like he asked them to? He explicitly gave them instructions of where to go and which path to follow. He didn't stray far from the path, even when he chased the killer. The killer.

Fraser regrets tripping over the body. Had he been paying attention he could've avoided the boy caught his killer and brought him and the past children to justice. Everything could've been solved if he's been faster, competent, and not a huge lump of disappointment. O well, there were enough kids for him to have a chance to catch the killer. If Fraser cared about his thought process he would've slapped himself for that last thought.

He was surprised he was taking everything so well actually, at the moment he didn't feel anything, not a thing. It was oddly comforting.

"It seems I'll have to move you myself."

Before Fraser could process what was happening the cop grabbed him and dragged him out the woods into the back of the police car.

"Wait!"

The officer was just about to close the door to the cop car.

"I never got your name."

The cop deadpanned.

"Doug." And slammed the door shut.

It caused Fraser to jump before bursting into a fit of giggles. Doug. That's such a name
for a douchebag cop. It fitted perfectly. Perfectly perfect.

Fraser burst into another fit of giggles. Something told him he was heading very quickly
towards hysterics but he pushed the thought so far back in his head, it bordered on unreachable.

It was with everything else Fraser couldn't bare to face at the moment, though the space was
getting crowded.

Doug didn't get in the driver's seat, but another cop did, it was the one that could get beat up by the wind. Doug stalked back to the woods going the wrong way it seemed. Fraser laughed and turned his attention to the cop in the front seat.

"Hi I'm Fraser," he introduced. "What's your name?"

The cop in question looked at Fraser in distaste. It was obvious he wanted nothing to
do with Fraser. So he ignored him.

"What," Fraser asked. "I don't bite."

He sneezed noisily and sniffed up the upcoming wave of snot. Whatever he couldn't sniff
up he wiped on his sleeve. The snot glistened on the cuff.

The cop watched it through the rearview mirror and grimaced. Fraser caught the look and
smiled.

"I might be contagious," he laughed.

The cop continued to be disgusted and Fraser continued to lose his mind, all the while
thinking he was just in a silly goofy mood.

The passenger door opened and Doug plopped in. The two dupes, taking away
the bad guy.

Fraser put a hand over his mouth to stop the giggles

that threatened to pour out. The cops
caught the action and exchanged looks, starting the long
ride to the police station.

When they arrived at the police station Fraser
wouldn't get out of the car. It took two cops to get him
from the backseat, as he grappled at everything that could
keep him from the station. He didn't want to go back
and be interrogated by Chief Henry, didn't want his Aunt
Kimberly to have to come back and suffer the knowledge
that her nephew is forever entwined with death.

He knew he was acting a bit weird, but he couldn't
seem to care. It was all too much for him. The dead
children, his mysterious father, his withering aunt, lack
of sleep, the nightmare, everything was too much. His
brain had stopped processing and now he's left to fend for
himself without a brain. It was as if his body was going
to implode, even under his skin was crawling with the
emotions that couldn't stay in his heart, or find room to
float through his blood stream or get worked out in his
brain.

Fraser wanted to step backwards into time where he
wasn't born.

"Welcome back Fraser, though I wish I could say
that under better circumstances."

The cops had set him back in the room with the
double sided mirror and metal furniture. Chief Henry sat
across from him once again.

Fraser ignored him and looked at the concrete. They
could've covered it with carpet or
wood paneled floor. It would look more presentable.

Fraser.

That woman's voice.

"Go away."

Chief Henry gave Fraser a sideways look before
glancing around the room.

You need to wake up.

"I am awake."

Chief Henry looked around the room one more time.

Face reality.

"Shut up!"

"Fraser!" Chief Henry slammed his palms on the table, startling Fraser. He looked at Fraser as if he grew another head. All this talking made his temples throb.

"I'm okay," he breathed.

"You don't seem okay."

He was right.

Fraser looked up at the mirror and focused on himself.

Sleep-deprived, dehydrated, malnourished. He looked like his mom the night she died.

He couldn't even shiver in fear. Mid shiver he sneezed and went in a coughing fit that even had the Chief backing up.

"Let's get this over with," Chief Henry said. "So we can get you some help."

Fraser shook his head.

"I don't need help," Fraser sighed. "I'm just tired."

Tired was an understatement. Drained and burn-out seemed more fitting than tired. Rightfully,

Chief Henry gave a meanful look to the mirror behind him before turning back to Fraser.

"How did you find the body?"

If Fraser said that he accidentally found the body would he believe him? Probably not. Maybe he could say he fell head over heels. It wouldn't be that far from the truth.

A stupid smile crossed Fraser's face.

"I lost something and went to the woods to find it."

Chief Henry looked like he didn't believe in that either.

"What were you so deep in the woods?"

Fraser didn't expect him to go along with it, though it helped his brain function again as he tried to pave the path of his story.

"A necklace." He didn't want to give any details yet.

Chief Henry's face twitched, fed up with how the story was going.

"Why would your necklace be in the woods? And what kind of necklace is it that you'd

try to find it in the forest?" He drawled.

Fraser's head hurt, whether from the abrupt thinking or lack of sleep, he didn't know.

"Liam and I were hanging out in the forest and as for the necklace it wasn't of importance really." He stated.

Chief Henry leaned in, interested in where the conversation was headed.

"Then why did you look in the woods for it," he asked, still skeptical. "You'd have to know you'd find it by a long shot."

"It had my dad's face on the front, I wanted to know more about it."

Chief Henry stood rigid. Fraser knew he would. There was no way a necklace belonging

to his mother would've been out in the woods for no reason.

"Did you find it," he asked carefully. "In the woods, I mean."

Fraser lied and shook his head.

"I couldn't find it at all and instead found a body, imagine how traumatizing that was." Fraser deadpanned.

The interrogation room door slammed open and Aunt Kimberly strolled red-faced and

angrier than a bull.

"Why was Fraser brought to the police," she demanded angrily. "Again."

Chief Henry got up, putting his hands up as if in surrender, his shoulders caving in.

"He was at another crime scene, and he called the police."

Aunt Kimberly walked over to Fraser and pulled him close to her chest.

"You know good and well that Fraser isn't the killer."

Fraser watched, shocked as Chief Henry nodded.

"I do know that," he admitted softly. "But you also know he isn't completely innocent in this ."

She clutched him tighter to her chest causing his head to pound. He couldn't tell what was going on.

"If you ever have this boy in the police station by heaven. Keith Henry .I will show you my wrath."

If Fraser was feeling better and in the right state of mind he would've laughed at his aunt's childish threats.

"Kim you know I can't do that."

She ignored him and stepped back taking Fraser with her.

"We're leaving," she said. "Have a blessed day."

Fraser burst out laughing.

"What are you chuckling about," she asked, as they walked out the police station. He shook his head.

"You're a great person auntie."

For the first time in a while he gave her a genuine smile.

"O Fraser you're my everything."

While Fraser loved those words, they didn't filter properly. The love that was laced with it wasn't sinking in. Something really was wrong with him.

They got in the car and his aunt fussed over him non-stop.

"Aunt Kimberly."

She stopped mid-fuss and looked at her nephew.

The look on his face didn't warrant anything but complete seriousness.

"Does anyone know about the murders?"

A dumb question, but one that had been on his mind since he talked to Liam.

"Yes."

Fraser looked over at his aunt.

"If everyone knows why isn't there more noise? Like concerned people calling for outside help or a better way to protect the kids?"

The silence from his aunt told him Liam was right. The townspeople couldn't face the fact that someone in town was causing their kids harm.

They got home quickly and parted ways. It gave Fraser room to think, not that, that helped anyone. His thinking led nowhere. Liam however...

He was always so certain. He knew about the reason the killer wasn't found, the real reason Fraser wanted to catch the killer. He loved his aunt but Liam was right, it wasn't for her.There was no doubt in his mind. He needed to see Liam. Once again he was left without his car. Hopefully his aunt could get his car back, however, in the meantime... Fraser took her keys and got in her car driving off to a place isolated from the rest of the town.

Liam's house was originally his grandma's house who died from fatal injury, aftering falling down the stairs. It was a small cabin a little ways from the town itself, surrounded by trees. The perfect spot to remain unseen.

Fraser whipped out his phone and dialed a number before shoving it in his pocket and knocking on the door.

It took a minute before Liam opened it. He looked... normal. As if today was any other day as if there weren't murders happening just miles away.

"Another kid died," he deadpanned in greeting.

Liam stated, blinked and turned around, walking into the house.

He left the door open and Fraser used that as an invitation to come in.

"I texted you," Fraser said. "Why didn't you answer?"

He followed Liam to the dining room table though he didn't sit down. He stared at Liam and waited for him to answer.

"Is that your way of an apology?"

Fraser ignored the question.

Liam sighed.

"Why are you here?"

Finally a good question.

"You told me I had no sense in reality, that I knew nothing was going on around me." Liam nodded and sat back in his chair.

"What did you mean by that?"

"Fraser, you're an inspiration."

He blinked. Fraser hadn't ever expected that to come from his mouth or anyone's mouth for that matter.

"An inspiration," he said slowly. "What on earth would make you say that?"

"You can interact with the dead, help those go to peace-"

He knows

"Do you know what goes on behind closed doors Fraser?"

Something clicked into place.

"I don't," he said. "But why would you help me find the killer? You hate children."

Liam looked appalled.

"I could never," he said vehemently. "The children are all bundles of joy."

He could hear his aunt in that last phrase.

"How could you know? They're all locked up in their

houses because of the murders."

Liam rolled his eyes.

"Children will be children. They slip out now and then and play in the woods. I live in
the woods. Connect the dots."

He did. Fraser could feel everything slowly connecting itself.

"It took us a while to find where you were. We couldn't find you."

It was so obvious that it made Fraser's brain hurt to think it took forever to figure it out.

"Liam."

"Hm?"

"Where is your phone?"

"I lost it. Why?"

It took 20 minutes for the police to come, when he was in the forest earlier today. For 20 minutes Fraser tried to look everywhere for a clue about the killer. For once something went right. He found something black on the forest floor, something that the killer had dropped. Knowing that and knowing the police were useless he swiped the phone.

The question was random, one that would make Liam pause and look at him like he was weird.

Fraser shook his head and took a step back. Everything slowly seeped in.

"You already knew the little boy was dead, didn't you? I saw someone today, was it you?"

Liam's eyes widened, then relaxed until they closed.

"Liam?"

The person in question opened his eyes and stared at Fraser before bursting out laughing.

"Oh Fraser, you never should've come back."

The words Fraser wanted to say left him as

everything started to come at him. The hysteria that he held as a shield crumbled away. All the emotions he hid behind the questions, the giggles and peals of laughter, stabbed him like shards of ice. They choked him and Fraser went into a coughing fit.

"At first I wanted to see where your presence would go but now I wish I'd gotten rid of you when I had the chance."

His childhood friend was no more. Fraser was finally awake.

The woman's breath, he could feel it on his neck.

I told you so, didn't I?

She did. He just never thought it would be Liam.

Never trust everyone.

It was annoying how right she was. It was annoying how cold he was yet his skin was
layered in sweat. How his throat felt like it was closing up and oxygen was trying to abandon him. Fraser wheezed as darkness clouded his vision.

"This doesn't make sense."

You've done enough.

Invisible hands wrapped around his neck in a suffocating embrace.

Rest.

Fraser fainted.

sleep seem very short. Though he couldn't complain. His sleep was no longer plagued with nightmares but oddly realistic dreams. No more horror stories since Liam was locked up.

Liam was the killer, and at the time Fraser was surprised now he believes it was bound to happen. His whole story was just tragic.

His parents died before he could learn to walk and he was stuck living with his only relative, his grandmother. She raised him all while battling schizophrenia, though no one knew until she really lost it. She claimed Liam was the devil's advocate because he was friends with Fraser. Said Liam and Fraser would rule over the dead and kill off those who stood in their way.

She went so far as to try and kill him. Luckily it happened in front of the daycare and there was no serious threat to his life. Still, he was an orphan that no one volunteered to look after. Accept Fraser's aunt of course, but there was only so much she could do.

In the end he turned out to be a killer, a child killer no doubt. He was an unfortunate child
that turned out to be an awful adult who gave out misfortune to everyone around town. In a way
it was karma for how they ignored Liam, his pain, his struggles and the reality of his situation.

However, no one deserved to be murdered or have their loved one murdered. Losing a loved one was excruciating.

A knock on his door startled Fraser.

"Are you up?"

It was his aunt. Fraser sighed and sat up, he planned on sleeping just a bit longer.

"Yes," he called. "I'm up."

He heard his aunt hum in reply. She didn't have the heart to wake him up, not after the night terrors kept him from sleeping.

"Good, go ahead and get yourself together before I go to work."

Fraser smiled. It wasn't announced that Liam was the killer but because he was locked up at the police station, until he could get transferred, the town went to their own conclusions. In the town there aren't things that are announced, but people always find out. It was both a blessing and a curse since half of the time they're guessing and weren't always right.

It did however get Aunt Kimberly's job at the school back and that's really all that mattered, at least what Fraser told himself. Happy aunt, happy life.

Fraser pried himself from the bed and got into a necessary shower, making sure it was boiling hot to help clear his sinuses. It relaxed his muscles yet burned him at the same time. His bodily temperature had dropped alarmingly, another reason for the hot water. Fraser however wasn't worried about it, he chalked it down to the lot of cold showers and the fact that he was still sick.

By the time he was getting dressed he could smell the faint hint of what was for breakfast. His mouth watered and his nose twitched at the meaty aroma. Fraser quickened what he was doing and went down the stairs to the kitchen. He sat at the kitchen table, a plate of food waiting for him, the steam rising.

"Thanks for the food," he said and carefully sat down in the chair.

The plate was overflowed with food, bacon, eggs, fruit, french toast, hashbrown and sausage. He was afraid that if he touched or moved suddenly the plate would fall over.

He looked at his aunt in amazement.

"This is a little much."

His aunt blushed as she fixed her own plate.

"Sorry, I couldn't help myself."

Fraser didn't push the matter further because he knew why his aunt did it. After Fraser blacked out he woke up in urgent care with a high fever and a crying aunt. She fussed over him to the extreme until he was able to get home just two days ago.

He tried to eat as much of the food as he could before he was absolutely stuffed. Aunt Kimberly, glanced at him and then his food.

"I'm full," he announced, patting his stomach in emphasis.

Aunt Kimberly gave him a sideways glance.

"Just a few more bites," she pressed. "Please."

Fraser could never ignore his aunt when she said please.

Sighing, he picked up his fork and stabbed a piece of sausage. He looked at it for a moment in dread before shakily putting it in his mouth and chewing. As he swallowed he could've sworn he felt it stop just as it entered his stomach. He was more than full, he felt himself getting sick .

His aunt continued to look at him and he hurriedly scooped a forkful of eggs and shoved them in his mouth, chewing until the food was mush in his mouth before swallowing. Aunt Kimberly continued to look at him and Fraser looked at the time.

"Oh no," he deadpanned. "Gosh, look at the time."

Aunt Kimberly followed his direction and looked at the time displayed on the stove.

"Dear you're right," she said. "I'm almost late for work."

She got up and rinsed her plate in the sink before putting it in the dishwasher. Aunt Kimberly grabbed her keys and purse and was almost out the door when she stopped.

"You forgot something." Fraser looked at his aunt in wonder.

She went to stand a distance away from Fraser and did a little twirl, her curls bouncing. "How do I look?"

Since it was her first day back in a while she dressed up in a white floral dress and even put a white ribbon in her hair. Most importantly though, her eyes sparkled like the sun reflectingoff the sea.

"Beautiful," he whispered. "Absolutely stunning."

His Aunt Kimberly blushed and flicked her wrist. "O stop it."

Fraser laughed.

"You're gonna be late."

That got her jumping into action.

"You're right. I'll text you later."

The front door closed with a click and Fraser was left all by his lonesome. All that food had yet to digest and he didn't feel like exploring. A nap was in order, but that would cause him indigestion. Fraser sighed. What a dilemma.

He would watch TV for a few hours and then take a nap and wake up just in time to greet his aunt when she came home and they could have dinner together. Perfect plan. It deserved a pat on the back.

Except it didn't go to plan. Somehow he ended up watching *Good Girls* and after a few episodes it roped him in. He kept watching episode after episode, munching on snacks from the pantry and forcing himself not to fast forward to the end and having an unsatisfactory spoiler.

He kept up the Good Girls marathon until his aunt came in. Immediately he turned off the TV and tried to act natural. If his aunt caught him watching *Good Girls* he wouldn't hear the end of it.

"Welcome back," he greeted and Aunt Kimberly

jumped.

"Goodness gracious Fraser." She put a hand over her chest. "You scared me." Fraser laughed and sat up straight on the couch.

"Didn't expect me to be here? What's going on?"

Kimberly locked the door and threw her keys and placed her purse on the dining room table.

"I thought you'd be napping up in your room."

Fraser held his tongue. That's what he wanted to do before he got stuck on Good Girls.

"That's a good idea." He heaved himself off the couch with a groan. "I'll do that right now."

He stretched before hopping up the stairs. His aunt laughed at his energy.

"Alright, I'll call you when dinner's ready."

Fraser nodded and went inside his room, throwing himself on the bed.

"I've missed you," he said, voice muffled.

Of course the bed didn't respond but its blankets were warm as if welcoming him. Since he had a hearty meal and had been putting off his nap. It was to no one's surprise he was out like a light.

Even his naps were plagued with the dead. The graveyard sky was bright as it truly was outside and it threw him for a bit of a loop. It revealed more details, more graves then there were originally.

Oscar Jameson, stood by his gravestone next to two others. Fraser did a double-take. He could've sworn the area was just empty space.

He walked over to the gravestones and kneeled down. There were no names, dates, or any type of engraving. They were just two slabs of rock. Was it a fluke?

Either way, it was unsettling. He couldn't find the answer to the question he sought and he didn't know if he wanted the answer. Fraser would get it, however, whether he wanted to or not. He sighed. It was probably just there for decoration.

Bouncy curls brushed his shoulders and itched his neck. Fraser couldn't move.

You know...

He tried to crane his neck but his neck was a stone pillar, unable to move. Though he already guessed it was that woman, the one who helped guide him along, so he didn't make a total fool of himself.

The warm breath that heated up the hair on his neck caused it to burn.

...I lied.

Fraser whirled around to open air. She was nowhere to be seen. What did she mean when said she lied? About what?

He shrugged off her words and turned back towards the twin slabs of rock, trying to think of what it meant.

His eyes took in the sight and it clicked. No, no, NO!

Fraser woke up screaming.

XII

Aunt Kimberly didn't check on Fraser after he screamed. She wasn't there. She got a call from a devastated mother, dealing with the loss of a child and left the house in a hurry. Covered in sweat, Fraser gasped for breath and tried to regain his composure.

He wiped his hands up his face and through his hair. He took deep breaths and counted backward from one hundred in his head. Focusing on something, anything other than the endless tragedy, the grief that came from the string of dead kids would calm him down.

He caught the killer, he knew he did, yet his dreams said otherwise. Nonetheless that's what they were. Just dreams. They wouldn't be dreams if it was real. Fraser nodded with that logic and got up and took another shower. It was too warm, and his body couldn't function properly under such temperatures.

Fraser decided to do his whole morning routine over, needing something to do. Brushing his teeth and washing his face, picking out a whole new outfit and when he finished he went downstairs and to the kitchen.

"Aunt Kimberly..."

She wasn't in the kitchen. His aunt had told him she would be making dinner. Where was she?

He called his aunt a few more times before he saw her purse and keys missing. She had left. Why didn't she tell him, he wondered. Even if she was in a hurry she would pop her head in and tell him or at least give him a text or note to wake up to.

Fraser didn't have anywhere else to go and nothing else to do so he did the only thing he knew. Clean. Back home there wasn't a time Fraser wasn't tasked with cleaning. It wasn't peaceful or soothing for him, but it kept his body busy and it helped pass the time.

And so, Fraser cleaned upstairs: the three bedrooms (though one was locked), two bathrooms, and cleaned downstairs: the kitchen, living room and dining room. There wasn't much to clean since his aunt kept the house spick and span. All he needed to do was dust and straighten everything up. Most of the work he needed to do was clean up his own room. Fraser could clean up after himself everywhere but his room. It was kinda sad if you asked him, though he'd say it was because he was comfortable in his own space.

As Fraser wiped down the counters with a wet wipe, the final touch to him cleaning the kitchen his eyes seemed to wander down the hall. His aunt hadn't specifically said he wasn't allowed to go down there, but something told him he shouldn't, which is why he didn't. He wanted to know what was down there but he didn't want to invade his aunt's privacy when she'd done such a good job respecting him.

Still, his feet carried him down the hall and it ended and a single door was to his right.
Fraser assumed it was a basement but maybe it was something different. Something secretive. The last time he found something secret about his aunt was when she was eating cake when she went on her greens smoothie diet. He couldn't quelch the giddiness that he felt when he thought

of his aunt keeping a secret. Fraser was 100% certain that the secret was something minor like a hello kitty obsession and maybe some normal family snooping would make things better.

He wrapped his hand around the door handle and turned it until the door clicked open. It opened towards him and he moved to the side to take a peek at what was behind. A dark staircase looked back. Fraser cringed back a step. Stairs and darkness weren't something he sought out.

He went down the first stair and groped the walls on each side for a light switch. He eased down to the second stair and did the same. This continued until he got to the 5th stair and his hand brushed something. Fraser flicked the light up so fast the muscle surrounding his wrist twitched in pain.

Now confident about his movements Fraser ventured step by step down the stairs until his bare feet were plush against the carpeted floor. He looked around and was disappointed to see a washer and dryer and laundry baskets. It was an ordinary laundry room. Not giving up, Fraser looked around, behind the washing machine, behind the dryer and around the baskets full of laundry, nothing.

He gave up with a sigh. Fraser at least wanted to find something embarrassing, like a crush on some weird guy down the street or some naked baby picture his aunt wished was burned. No, he would find something on his Aunt Kimberly as if his life depended on it. His aunt couldn't be the type of person who cuddled him unquestioningly when he had a scary nightmare or fussed over him when he seemed the slightest bit unwell.

She couldn't be the person who sobbed because she couldn't play with the kids or who would badmouth someone before telling them to have a blessed day, without having something to hide His Aunt Kimberly couldn't be someone who was so normal when so far from it abnormal wasn't the right word.

For the next half hour Fraser was on all fours crawling around to see if there was a lift in the carpet or a hole in the wall, maybe a chip in the wallpaper he could rip away to reveal a hidden door. There were zero secrets, zilch. Bummer.

Fraser trudded his way upstairs and ready the house for a wide sweep. Maybe he could find something, anything that made her seem less...perfect. The stairs creaked underneath him and he hoped he wouldn't catch a splinter.

Something shiny under the stairs caught his eye. The stairs themselves were boards with space in between each one, a clumsy person could slip through the cracks and hurt themselves.

He leaned forward, making himself smaller so he could see under the stairs, when the front door slammed close. The basement light swung back and forth and Fraser fell forward smashing his head against the wooden stairs.

Blood singed on his taste buds as he bit his tongue to cover the sound he was going to let
out. Holding onto his head Fraser bounded up the stairs and grabbed the door handle, swinging the door open.

He tripped on the last stair and stumbled into the hall.

"Fraser?" His aunt called, concerned.

Fraser looked like a deer caught in the headlights. His eyes widened and his body stiffened.

His aunt stood with red eyes as she dropped her purse and keys on the living room couch.

"What are you doing," she asked.

He felt like he was treading on melting ice. He forced himself to straighten up and give a
a shaky smile.

"I was cleaning my room when I realized I lost one of my shirts. I knew you washed them, so I went downstairs to check, but I couldn't find it."

The lie slipped off his tongue with an ease that made his stomach turn. It took a while for Aunt Kimberly to process what he was saying and warning bells went off in his head.

"What happened," he asked.

His aunt had a faraway look in her eyes that scared him. Even more so than when she
was down in the dumps the time she was forced to leave her job. They looked void of life.

"They were in the middle of town," she said. "Everyone saw them."
Fraser's brows dipped in confusion

"Who was in the middle of town?"

Aunt Kimberly's eyes glazed over with tears and her face crumpled.

"The twins," she cried. "They were murdered."

The world tilted and in an instant turned dark.

Once more, he was staring at the gravestones next to Charles. Except there were details on them.

George and Peter Henderson
Sons, Brothers, and Friends
Cherished by All

Fraser saw two pairs of feet standing next to the combined graves and couldn't bear to lift his eyes. He stared at the ground, his vision became blurry as he tried to hold his tears back. He caught the wrong one. Liam wasn't the killer. He made everyone relax, he killed the twins. He killed George and Peter Henderson.

Fraser fell to the ground as the dam behind his eyes broke and his cheeks were rained down with tears.

"I'm sorry," he sobbed. "I'm so, so, sorry."

They didn't accept or reject his apology, just stared.

However, not everyone was like them.

"Why didn't you get the bad man?"

He sniffled and finally looked up. It was Charlotte.

"I..." Fraser didn't know how to respond.

"Can you catch the bad man that killed us?" It was Charles, he was crying. "My mom and dad would be sad if they knew the bad man wasn't put on punishment."

Fraser shook his head.

"I-I'm afraid I don't know how." He looked at his hands, they were shaking.

"Will you listen to her story?"

Fraser looked back up at the kids.

"Who's story?"

"My story."

Fraser turned around at the voice and blinked. The woman, who he thought was helping

him and lied to him, was still a child. A teenager, she couldn't be a second older. Fraser gritted

his teeth. It was her fault he had his friend arrested, she practically framed him.

"How do I know if your story's true?"

The girl crossed her arms over her chest.

"I've been 14 years old for 32 years, I was born to a teen mom."

Fraser could already feel himself withdrawing from her story.

"There were no complications with the birth except the father didn't want to be part of our lives, my life."

Resentment coated her words.

" In such a small town, everyone knew about my mom's pregnancy no matter

how much she tried to hide it. She was ridiculed and when they knew the father wouldn't be in our lives got even worse. I was born in a world of hatred."

"Growing up adults would talk about me, gossiped

loudly when they thought I couldn't hear them, and whispered when they thought I could. My mom was already going through so much, being outcast. I couldn't burden her by telling her what was really going on."

That was the only part Fraser could heavily relate to. For a moment he felt for her, wanted to help her, before he remembered the trouble she had caused.

"As I got older I thought I got used to it until I met the one person I harbored hatred for my whole life. My father. I knew who he was, my mother kept her lips sealed with anything

involving him, but it was hard to keep secrets in such a small town. I bumped into him, finally, I got to see him and he glared at me. He said, 'watch where you're going' and 'try not to bump into strangers.'"

She choked on the word and gasped on its release, yet Fraser was unaffected.

"He abandoned me and pretended as if I didn't exist as he waltzed around town. Never even defended me when I knew for a fact he heard what they were saying about mother and me. I

couldn't do it."

Tears streamed down her face.

"I couldn't keep growing up in a town where every corner was pain and suffering. Kids' and mine and future generations grew up avoiding me, hating me, bullying me for something out of my control. But mother didn't want to leave the town behind, it was all she knew. So I left the only way I could."

She hesitated, tears starting to sober up.

"I took my mother's pills and swallowed one, then another and another. I thought it was a peaceful way to die, but it was a lie. It hurt so bad, the excruciating, agonizing pain, I felt as if my stomach was twisting itself into little knots until my organs would explode. On instinct I tried to

vomit it up, make the pain go away but I clenched my teeth and held my lips tightly together. I couldn't breathe, oxygen just wouldn't come into my lungs and I could feel my lungs stop expanding, my blood stop flowing until my heart stopped. It took 2 and a half hours but I finally made it, to the world of the dead."

The girl took a few moments to collect herself and Fraser shoved his trembling hands in his pocket.

"Well since you told me your story," Fraser said sarcastically. "Wanna tell me your name?"

"I have more to say," she said.

Fraser let out a shaky sigh, his head needed to stop hurting.

"Okay then," he paused and took a deep breath. "Tell me your name first and then the rest of your story."

She wiped her tears and told him her name.

Fraser could feel his world crashing down around him.

He opened his eyes and sat up. His chest heaved up and down as he caught his breath. It took a few moments to realize he was no longer in his bedroom. Fraser scrambled to his feet and jerked his head side to side.

"No," his voice cracked. "No, no, this isn't real."

The grass was like shards under his feet and stone slabs of death surrounded him. He was in the graveyard. Taking his skin between finger tips he pinched the hell out of himself. Still there he was in the graveyard. The dreams that he thought were guilty conscious were real. Fraser willed himself to faint, yet darkness avoided him. It couldn't be real.

His ringtone played loudly causing him to jump. Not taking his eyes off his surroundings, he shakily pulled out his phone and answered the call.

"Hello?"

"You know who the real killer is now?"

Fraser stumbled.

"L-Liam?"

Liam sighed in exasperation

"Do you know where the evidence is?"

"I...need to talk to someone first."

"While you do that I'll head to the house, there's something I need to give to you. Meet me in the forest in 30 minutes."

Liam hung up the phone and Fraser stood there speechless.

Go.

The wind roared in his ear.

Fraser started down a dreaded path.

XIII

There's a story about a cabin in the woods; perfectly isolated from the rest of town; however, any path taken could lead to any part of the town. All without having to leave the woods, it was perfect to walk around unseen, to be inconspicuous.

But that's not the only thing unique about it. Underneath that roof lived a beautiful three-generation family, until the grandfather passed away from old age and things started to spiral out of control. The grandmother was slowly losing her memories, her morals, her mind. There was only so much her son and daughter-in-law could handle. They knew the only way they could be free was to leave their son behind, his grandmother adored him, and would never let him leave her sight.

When the time came to execute their plan, they left when the moon had just touched the sky and the grandmother, grandson duo were in bed, they left. Fate, however, never approved of the parent's cruelty. They died before they could reach the airport. A deer jumped out on the road at the last minute. Their death didn't reach the town until several weeks later by curious townsfolk who wanted to ask the airport whether they really left town.

They did–just not the way they wanted to. Their son was left all alone with his senile grandma who tortured the poor boy with her sense of time that had long gone out of whack until she too died. She slipped and fell down the stairs. At least that was the story. For a while a rumor spread that the boy did it, he just couldn't handle his grandma any more and pushed her down the stairs. After a while it died down until it was vaguely whispered from time to time.

It was ironic he later grew up to be arrested for the childhood murders.

Withdrawing from their hiding place among the trees the killer stalked towards the cabin door, their steps light. They stopped just inches in front of the cabin door and just stood there. There were no sounds coming from within the cabin but they knew better. Liam was there. He probably sensed the killer from a mile away, the moment they staked out in the woods. They carefully turned the knob and gently pushed the door open. It swung open soundlessly. He had put oil in the hinges. Smart boy.

The killer looked around before taking their first steps inside. As abandoned as the cabin looked on the outside, it looked quite taken care of on the inside. All around was cleanliness, not a speck of dust anywhere.

The killer finished their observations and stepped further inside the house, the floorboard creaked underneath them. Had the killer not sensed him, Liam probably would've gotten away. They don't turn around, but slowly inched their way forward.

"You know...don't you?"

There was no reply in response but the killer knew he was listening.

"It wasn't just you who knew either, it was your grandmother who told you."

They could hear Liam, shuffling.

"Your grandmother was crazy but she was smart. She knew all along."

He was advancing, the killer knew it. Their hair was standing up on end and goosebumps spread down their arms and legs. The boy had an intent to kill. They could simply feel the upcoming threat.

"It's too bad she died before she could say anything."

The sound of a weapon whistling through the air had never felt so alive.

Turning around, the killer grabbed the baseball bat with one hand and with the other grabbed at the weapon they've been concealing the whole time. They pulled the trigger and shot Liam at blank range. He fell like a sack of potatoes. If he wasn't a liability, he could've continued living his life as the social outcast. If anything, the killer was doing him a favor. They walked over Liam's body and left the cabin. It was really the House of Tragedy.

XIV

Fraser's steps were so heavy. It felt like his feet were made of lead and his legs of stone.It took a while for Fraser to walk home. The door was unlocked and he hoped it wasn't. If it was locked he wouldn't have to cross the line.

He trudged straight to the basement and looked down at the darkness, it no longer phased him, numbness beginning to take over as he trudged down the stairs and stopped halfway. He already knew where to look, it was only for a second he gazed at it but found it engraved itself in his mind. Fraser turned around and bent down, shoulder brushing the stairs. The key was attached underneath the stairs with a piece of tape.

Fraser clawed at it irrationally, not wanting to know what door the key would unlock. Yet the tape that held it down and broke from its hiding place and fell in his hand. He gripped the key tightly in his hand as he got up and lumbered up the stairs.

That day when he was cleaning, he cleaned his room thoroughly and didn't do anything but straighten up his aunt's room. Fraser tried to do the guest room but it was locked. He thought nothing of it.

He stood in front of the guest bedroom and looked

down at the key in his palm. It was a gold key, not a hint of rust or age insight. Fraser positioned the key and hoped it didn't fit in the keyhole. It did.

Fraser took a deep breath before he pushed the door open. It was a bedroom. That much was obvious. It looked like the room of a middle schooler. Fuchsia pink walls, pink bed sheets, even a pink alarm clock. He was surprised the carpet wasn't pink.

Come in.

Ever since that dream, he could see them. The dead. He got short glimpses here and there. Now, it felt like a real person was standing next to him. Dead people don't look like dead people. They look like regular people and that's the scary part.

Come on Fraser

He hesitated before stepping into the room.

He looked around jumping when little Charlotte appeared.

"You scared the mess out of me."

Charlotte didn't seem to care. Instead, she walked over to the bed and sat on it.

Smoothing the pillow back Fraser could see something peeking from underneath. He walked over and followed the clue the little girl keyed to and pulled on it. A little red ribbon. It was tattered, but Charlotte's name embroidered on it is what brought his attention.

"No."

Charles appeared and kneeled next to a small box, a toy dinosaur was on top.

"Stop."

Peter and George walked into the room and stood behind Charles making airplane noises.
Fraser took a few steps closer and saw the paper airplanes hiding behind the large dinosaur.

"I'm not supposed to be here." Fraser told himself.

"I need to get out of here."

Fraser

That woman. It was all the women's fault.

"Stop talking to me."

Fraser

He shook his head, his previous numbness being chased away and took a step back.

"I thought I could go down this road but I can't."

Fraser please

Deny. Deny. Deny. Deny. Deny. Deny everything.

Just one more thing and then you can walk away.

He doesn't know what it was. The absolute defeat in her voice or his self-consciousness knowing that he had to face it, instead his feet moved. One step after another, until he was standing in front of the nightstand next to her. A picture frame face down.

Pick it up

I guess that answered the question of whether or not the dead could pick up objects. If

they could, Fraser might've joined them.

Pick it up Fraser

He didn't want to. He didn't want to see the picture. Yet his hands still inched toward it until he found his shaky hands gripping the picture frame and lifting it up. That woman stood next to someone with a wild head of curly blonde hair. Someone with sun-kissed skin, a bright cheery smile, and shining blue eyes. Someone that looked like his Aunt Kimberly.

"Are you sure that's your mom?" Fraser whispered. "You look nothing like her."

Nothing.

Fraser looked up. Everyone was gone. The children and that woman. No. Someone was behind him.

"Oh Fraser."

His fight or flight response was broken. Neither

happened. All at once, his muscles tensed until one of them spasmed yet he couldn't move. Even his heart seemed to stop and his blood stopped circulating.

"I loved you most and yet I can't keep you."

He couldn't hear her steps on the carpeted floor but he could feel her getting closer. For the first time in his life, his aunt caused his hair to stand up, causing fear to grip his spine.

"I..."

Fraser didn't know what to say. His aunt was the killer.

"Aunt Kimberly please."

Tears gathered in his throat before they made it to his eyes.

"You'll be the last one I promise."

The room fogged with his emotions. It weighed him down. Betrayal tore at his chest, until there was a gaping hole ready for someone to rip his heart out. And it was, when the killer slammed a trophy against the back of his head and plunged him into darkness.

He was awake but his eyes were closed. In books and movies, when you're kidnapped it's better for the kidnapper to think you're incapacitated so they can let their guard down and the kidnappee can get their bearings together. Though no matter what, Fraser wasn't going to be able to stop his mind from breaking into tiny little pieces. He's trying to glue them back together so they could function and find a way to end this mess but to do that he would have to wage war against his Aunt Kimberly. The one that was there for him when he didn't want to be there for himself. Yet here he was.

In what he thought was a car. He heard the engine and felt as if they were moving fast yet slow at the same time. Maybe he could reach the car door and fall out without his aunt noticing.

Then he could run to the airport and never come back.

"I know you're awake."

Since she knew, Fraser didn't see any point in hiding the truth and opened his eyes. His aunt was a wreck. A bigger one than when Charlotte died and even bigger than when the twins died. Murdered. When they were murdered.

It wasn't knotted hair, the crumpled clothes, and the messed up makeup. It was her eyes. They were red and kept shaking like they couldn't focus. The word wreck didn't do the look justice.

"Aunt Kimberly," he whispered. "You murdered those kids, didn't you?"

He watched as his aunt looked down at the wheel before putting her eyes back on the road.

"I helped them."

Fraser shook his head.

"You killed them, auntie."

She paused. It had been a long time since he called her that.

"I saved their lives."

Fraser put weight in his arms to sit up and realized his hands were bound. He shimmied up into a sitting position.

"You took them from their families."

Kimberly shook her head crazily, her curls sticking to her face.

"You don't know what was happening Fraser," she stated. "On the outside, they were happy families with smart children and caring parents but they were lies."

Fraser's brow furrowed as he tried to adjust to having his wrist tied together.

"What were lies?" He asked, his face twisting in concentration.

"The parents didn't love their children," she blurted, eyes crinkling as she tried to hold back tears. "Charlotte's parents starved her. I couldn't let her go through that. Children naturally have tummies, it goes away with age, not with starvation." Fraser knew that sometimes the parents in the town weren't the best of parents but to starve them was unthinkable.

"And Charles poor Charles they beat that boy silly whenever they got home. His father was drunk and his mother wallowed in self-pity and couldn't seem to keep her hands off the boy even if she tried. She was so angry at her life that she decided to ruin her sons."

He didn't want to hear her anymore. Those kids that were signaling to his aunt's trophies never had a good life. And for his aunt to end it just like that. Fraser couldn't view it as a blessing but as a tragic end. He couldn't help himself asking.

"The twins?"

Kimberly's lip wobbled as her cheeks grew aflame.

"Peter and George were known for their looks, they were handsome to a fault. Everyone one knew that but it was their older sister who knew it most. Every night she made them play little games. Simon Says was a popular one. 'Simon says take off your shorts.' 'Simon says, take off your underwear.'"

Fraser could feel his stomach burn.

"It got worse and worse every night and the parents knew. Can you believe it?" No he couldn't.

"How do you even know all this," he asked. "Were you spying on your victims before you killed them?"

Kimberly shook his head and gave Fraser a pitying look, furrowing her brows and pouting her lips.

"You want me to be the bad guy so bad, don't you, Fraser?"

Fraser didn't speak. He could feel his throat closing

up.

"The kids told me. Charlotte kept saying how hungry she was, how weird it was to be able to have so much food during snack time. Every time the kids would go out to play Charles would always stay behind. When I asked him he would say it hurts. It wasn't until I helped him change that I saw just why it hurt. He said he fell, that he bruised easily. A child could fall off a cliff and walk it off not once saying they're in pain and the twins.... Oh, they didn't know how they felt when their loathsome, despicable sister did those disgusting things to them and they tried to do them to other kids. I knew it then but it wasn't until I brought it up to the parents and they brushed it off that I knew everything."

If Kimberly shook her head any more, Fraser felt it would fall off.

"The kids were in so much pain I couldn't stand by and watch when everyone in town ignored it."

"So-," Fraser pushed back the tears piling in his throat. "Why not kill the parents?"

Kimberly blinked, once, twice.

"Had the kids lived they would've grown up worse than their parents."

Fraser couldn't stop the whimper that vibrated his chest and made tears burn trails down his cheeks. His aunt had really lost her mind. Her nephew hoped that she had a really good reason for ending those children's lives. Hoped that maybe it was good enough to sweep it under the rug as crazy as that sounded. Something that justified his aunt's actions, his aunt's crimes. But there was no excuse for murdering a child.

"Was it because of your daughter," Fraser asked. "She killed herself because of the people of the town."

Kimberly's face warped as her lips peeled away in a snarl.

"She killed herself because of *him*."
Raw hatred oozed from her being and almost dried the tears on his cheeks.

"I made my realization when you were born Fraser."
Time was suspended. Fraser was three seconds from mentally checking out. Dead kids, dead cousin, murderer aunt. It was all his fault.

"You were born in the world of the dead."
Fraser shook his head.

"That's- tha-." He gasped, not able to finish his words.

"Your parents loved you dearly, they looked forward to every moment they would spend with you."
Stop.

"But you were a stillborn. There weren't any cries, just silence and a baby with no healthy flush. You came into the world dead. Your mother was devastated."
Please.

"Yet somehow the doctor resuscitated you, you were alive Fraser."
She had the nerve to laugh and Fraser sunk his teeth into his lip, wishing so bad that he didn't come back to town.

"Your parents were good people and raised you to be a wonderful person."

"No more," he whispered brokenly. "Please, this is madness."

"You were born to the dead, you helped the dead when you were little. You put them to rest. You made me realize Fraser that good parents produce good kids that grow up and become great adults. That I need to take away those kids from bad parents so they won't become terrible adults."

Kimberly looked so happy at her realization. His aunt was gone. Fraser felt his chest burn as his heart broke.

"You know Kimberly," he began as a cool wave washed over him. "Your daughter forgave you for being a distant mom and not being able to protect her. The children...they forgive you for taking away their life before it even started but I-I can never forgive you."

Cold hands snapped his zip ties, his bond with the dead had grown stronger than ever.

"I don't expect you to forgive me Fraser," Kimberly spoke softly, her eyes in a dream like daze. "After all you were supposed to be my only victim."

It was like he was zapped, his arms whipped from behind him and he grabbed the wheel. In a split sec decision he yanked the wheel into the woods. Kimberly was screaming, trying to pull back onto the road, however, fate had other plans as they crashed straight into a tree.

Epilogue

The dead claimed no victims in the accident.

Knowing everything Liam had the ambulance and cops surrounding the scene minutes after it happened. Kimberly was arrested all while Fraser watched, eyes void of emotion as he went in and out of consciousness.

Kimberly was unharmed but Fraser had a blow to the head. For three weeks he was in bed with a coma with Liam playing as nurse maid. He talked to Fraser, told him how he missed him and how he was sorry for how he acted, he kept him updated on his aunt, how she was found guilty and would be transported to a prison a few towns over.

After Kimberly's arrest multiple things came to light. The town knew Kimberly was the killer since the beginning and they also knew that Fraser was the beginning of her twisted deeds. They pushed him out praying with him gone the murders would stop and they did, they just didn't expect Fraser to come back.

After what happened to her daughter the town's guilt made them lose their sense of self preservation. It was a mass of emotions, some blamed for her abominable crimes, while others couldn't help but feel like they created the monster she became, they didn't know whether to feel anger or guilt.

His father died of a broken heart. He knew of his aunt's dwellings but never thought she would go to jail, never thought she would get caught. It seemed mental illness was something running in the family as he didn't care about his sisters misdoings, even helped her position and drag bodies here and there. It was that his sister was going to be in jail, away from him, even if he moved near the jail, he couldn't see her without chains. It wasn't the same, the thought of change broke his heart. The lady next door almost had a heart attack finding him.

All the children's funerals were held together. It was the first time in a long time that parents leaned on each other, when it got too much, and shared their tears. A parent found his knees couldn't hold his grief and parents alike held him up. It was a beginning and repairing that family bond they had once lost. He missed everything and nothing at the same time. Liam made sure of that.

"I'm sorry for your loss."

Fraser stared down at his father's grave. He was the first one to visit his grave. Kimberly wasn't able to visit but she mourned his death loudly. Her wails could be heard from the police station.

"Are you," Fraser asked plainly.

Chief Henry looked down at Andrew's grave with regret. "Your father was like a brother to me," he said. "And your aunt- your aunt was like a-"

Fraser swung his gaze and stared at Chief Henry with cold eyes. "Don't you dare even say her name."

Henry swallowed with difficulty. "Listen I loved her-"

"No you didn't," Fraser stated."If you did none of this would've happened."

He wasn't saying the words out of anger or sport, it was the cold hard truth. Had Chief Henry loved Kimberly and their daughter like he was supposed to, everyone would've had a happy ending.

They respected Chief Henry even back then and would bend over backwards for him, that much hadn't changed.

Henry sighed, a deep sigh and looked back down at his best friend's grave.

"I know," he said softly. "I'll make it better."

Fraser's eyes narrowed his eyes in scrutiny as he examined the Chief's gaze. It was one he recognized. It was the look he tried not to give Kimberly when he felt all hope he was lost. It made him angry.

Gently, Fraser put the flowers down on his father's grave before turning around and snatching the Chief up by the collar.

"You will not follow my father to the grave."

He leaned close enough for their noses to touch and the faint scent of alcohol brushed his senses.

"You will live on in this town for the rest of your days and clean up the mess that you started."

Chief Henry's eyes widened in fear as he watched dangerous emotions darken Fraser's eyes.

"Because everything is just the beginning."

ABOUT THE AUTHOR

Madison Mcpherson was born in the state of Maryland but raised in Virginia, the state for lovers. She's a graduate of the Creating Writing Program at Charles J. Colgan Sr. High School and a future undergraduate at Nova majoring in Nursing. Madison is striving towards a career in nursing before fulfilling her dream of being a travel nurse. Obsessed with the art of travel, Madison aspires to travel around the world while balancing school and personal life. Madison is currently in the midst of publishing an upcoming fantasy romance novel in 2024.